CAPTIVE CAPTAIN

Kirk had the sensation of being lifted clear of the ground, experienced that peculiar sense of helplessness one has when one's feet no longer have contact with anything solid.

That was a common enough experience in free-fall space, but highly disconcerting on solid ground.

Then he turned and looked behind him and saw *what* had picked him up as neatly as an elephant plucks a lone peanut. He was in the grasp of the tail end—he supposed it could be the front end—of a creature some six or seven meters in length.

Whatever it was that had control of him, Kirk quickly discovered, was interested in keeping him intact and reasonably healthy . . .

**Also by Alan Dean Foster on the
Ballantine Books list:**

STAR TREK LOG ONE
STAR TREK LOG TWO
STAR TREK LOG THREE
STAR TREK LOG FOUR
STAR TREK LOG FIVE
STAR TREK LOG SIX
STAR TREK LOG SEVEN
MIDWORLD
LUANA
THE TAR-AIYM KRANG
ICERIGGER
DARK STAR
BLOODHYPE

STAR TREK LOG EIGHT

Alan Dean Foster

Based on the Popular Animated Series Created
by Gene Roddenberry

BALLANTINE BOOKS • NEW YORK

For REECE and CONNIE WOOLFOLK
For BEATRICE MURPHY
They don't say much about it, but their kind
of people built this country.

Library of Congress Catalog Card Number: 74-8477

ISBN 0-345-25141-5-150

Manufactured in the United States of America

First Edition: August 1976

Cover art supplied by Filmation Associates

STAR TREK LOG EIGHT

Log of the Starship *Enterprise*

Stardates 5537.1–5537.2 Inclusive

James T. Kirk, Capt., USSC, FC, ret.

Commanding

transcribed by
Alan Dean Foster

At the Galactic Historical Archives
on S. Monicus I
stardated 6111.3

For the Curator: JLR

THE EYE
OF THE
BEHOLDER

(Adapted from a script by David P. Harmon)

I

"Captain's log, stardate 5537.1. The *Enterprise* is embarked, for a change, on a routine follow-up mission—to search for a survey ship overdue for report-in in the vicinity of Epsilon Scorpii, last known to be investigating the system of a G4 sun designated Lactra on Federation starcharts."

He clicked off and studied the nearing globe and the yellowish, slightly hot sun beyond. The world and its star were no different from hundreds he'd examined personally or on tape. Yet past experience had shown that the innocuous-appearing worlds were often the ones full of surprises—planet-sized paranoia-inducing *piñatas*.

The continuing silence of the survey crew the *Enterprise* was here to locate *could* be due to some easily explainable equipment failure or minor human error. Could be.

But Kirk was a veteran starship captain, and he always wore two uniforms on such missions: Starfleet regulation pull-ons and an intense, personal wariness.

At the moment there was nothing to hint that Lactra VII was anything other than the recently discovered, inoffensive world it appeared to be. Only the small, obviously artificial shape growing slowly and silently larger on the main screen suggested otherwise.

The vessel was a long-range limited scout, of a minor class designed for extensive exploration of possible colonial worlds. It carried a small crew of first-contact xenologists and no frills, moving at high speed on an unvarying course from starbase to eventual destination. Its large quantity of complex instrumentation was announced by the bristling array of antennae, external sensor pickups, and other intricate detection equipment which almost obliterated the small hull.

Kirk noted with satisfaction that the scout looked undamaged. That probably ruled out any messy natural disasters such as meteorite collision and, more important, interference from some inimical spacegoing race. "Disarm phasers, Mr. Sulu," he instructed the helmsman.

"Phasers disarmed, sir."

The captain leaned toward the chair pickup and activated the log again. "Captain's log, supplemental. We have encountered and visually observed the missing survey ship. It continues to maintain communications silence." Glancing backward, he noted Lieutenant Uhura's confirming nod. All attempts to elicit some response from the craft had failed, though she continued trying.

"There is no evidence of violent damage or sentient attack. Mr. Spock will lead a security team in boarding the ship. End entry." Shutting off the recorder once again, he addressed another grid: "Transporter Room?".

"Chief Kyle here, Captain. Boarding party standing by."

"All right, Chief, send them aboard." He glanced backward. "Lieutenant Uhura, pick up visual and aural transmission as soon as transportation is complete."

"Standing ready, sir."

There was a tense pause, and then the view forward changed to an internal view of the scout. Kirk could see armed security personnel moving about as someone's visual scanner played around the ship's interior.

"Boarding party has integrated, Captain," a voice announced clearly . . . Spock's. "Our sensors were correct. Ship appears pressurized normally, temperature likewise."

The view shifted jumpily. Spock was walking through the cabin. "We are dispersing throughout the vessel, Captain."

"Any sign of life?" Kirk asked anxiously.

"Negative. There is ample evidence of previous tenancy, though. It looks as if the crew fully expected to return. There is nothing to indicate they were surprised, or removed forcibly from the ship. Personal effects are lying neatly about. There is no indication that the crew intended to leave their ship for an extended period."

"Very well, Mr. Spock. Continue your exploration."

Several hours sufficed to show that the only living things left on board the survey ship were laboratory animals. Automatic feeders kept them healthy in the absence of the crew.

Spock did make one important discovery, however.

"Captain, Dr. McCoy," he began as they watched expectantly from around the small table in the Briefing Room, "we found this tape lying in the ship's library, next to the playback slot. There is a duplicate in the ship's banks, but this copy was deliberately placed in a prominent position, obviously to attract the attention of anyone entering the library."

He picked up the small cassette and slid it into a slot set in the table, then depressed the play switch. Attention was focused now on the three-sided viewer which popped up in the table's center.

The tape showed a tense, worried officer in the uniform of Federation Sciences. He was staring into the pickup.

"It is now thirty-two minutes since our last contact with the three members of our crew who beamed down to the planetary surface," the man declaimed. "Each member of that crew was instructed to report in at ten-minute intervals.

"As this deadline has long since passed, and subsequent to our repeated failure to contact any member of the landing party, I have decided to take the following action. As senior officer aboard I, Lieutenant Commander Louis Markel, take full responsibility for this action and any consequences thereof." He coughed awkwardly, then continued on:

"All three remaining members of the survey team, myself included, will beam down in an attempt to discover the whereabouts of our comrades and, if necessary, to effect a rescue. If for any reason we should fail to return I, Lieutenant Commander Louis Markel, do hereby accept and acknowledge that—"

It was too much for Kirk. He jabbed the cancel switch and both picture and audio died. McCoy looked at him questioningly and saw that the captain was struggling to suppress a rising fury.

"What's the trouble, Jim?" he inquired quietly.

Kirk glared at him, the angry words tumbling over one another. "Blatant disregard of standard emergency procedure . . . utter suppression of survey orders! I tell you, Bones, there's no excuse for—"

"Apparently the lieutenant commander felt the need was pretty desperate, Jim," McCoy interrupted softly. "His friends had vanished, and he decided going after them was more important than anything else."

Kirk calmed down slightly, but McCoy could see the anger still simmering. "It doesn't matter, Bones. Letting personal feelings get in the way of Starfleet regs . . ." He sighed. "Since when were human beings otherwise?"

"True, Captain," commented Spock.

"Regulations specifically state, Bones, that in a situation like this at least two members of the crew—the minimum necessary to operate a ship this size—must remain aboard. In the event that contact with the other four team members is lost, they are to return to the nearest starbase beam region and file a full report. I don't care if the team commander is a full admiral. Regulations must be followed. They were created for a reason. Any sign of danger to Federation civilization . . ."

"But, Jim, there was no sign of danger," McCoy pointed out.

"That does not alter the fact, Doctor, that the survey ship's commander made what is essentially a personal decision," Spock observed.

Now it was McCoy's turn to explode. "Spock, you Vulcans are the most unimaginative, unbending . . . !"

"Easy, easy Bones," soothed Kirk. "You're starting to sound like me." He waited until McCoy had calmed himself, then continued briskly. "None of this is helping the situation any. Nor is it helping Commander Markel and his people—assuming they're still down there and in a position to make use of our help. Barring positive evidence to the contrary, we have to assume that they are."

"Sorry, Jim. Spock just has a way of getting to me sometimes." McCoy grinned. "It's an inborn talent, I guess."

Spock replied amiably, "Some humans are rather more easily gotten to than others, Doctor."

"Mr. Spock," Kirk continued, "what can we expect to find on Lactra Seven?"

"We have little information on the world below us," the first officer began thoughtfully. "What we do have is the result of the drone's preliminary report, coupled with information drawn from the survey ship's library. We may assume this basic information is fairly accurate. Our own sections are working to confirm this now.

"Lactra Seven is a Class-M world. Gravity is approximately Earth-normal, the atmosphere a reasonable analog of Earth-Vulcan. Very little additional useful information is on file. By useful I mean material which could aid in the locating and rescuing of the missing crew. What we do have is available in the printouts before you."

Kirk picked up the slim bundle of sheets and leafed through them. "According to the survey ship's log, Commander Markel and the other remaining members of his crew beamed down six weeks ago."

"Five weeks, three days, two hours, to be precise, Captain," Spock corrected.

"Careless of me, Mr. Spock." He finished scanning the printouts, then let the sheets drop. "No indication of planetary life forms."

'And in particular, of intelligent or large, dangerous ones—that is true, Captain," Spock admitted. "Life sensors are experiencing some difficulty in penetrating a distortion layer in the Lactran atmosphere.

"Given the composition of that atmosphere, the surface temperature, and the presence of large bodies of free water, I would suspect Lactra Seven harbors a considerable amount of life. But without additional data I cannot speculate on the form such life has taken." His brows drew together.

"Despite the distortion layer, the survey ship was specially equipped for obtaining just such information. Their records were surprisingly deficient in this area, one of primary concern to any survey team. Apparently they had no sooner entered into Lactran orbit when this emergency overwhelmed them. Mr. Arex is overseeing a full, detailed sensor scan, which should reveal the relevant information," he finished.

"Eventually," Kirk added. "Anything like a comprehensive scan will take too long to complete, Mr. Spock. Minutes might make the difference between life and death for Commander Markel and his people—if they're still alive. I want a landing party to beam down to the last recorded coordinates in the survey ship's tapes. If they've had the sense to remain in that immediate area we might be able to find them quickly."

"Don't you think that's taking an extreme risk, Jim?" put in McCoy. "If the first three were lost—and remember, they never beamed up any hint that something was wrong, no warning or anything—then we might run into the same silencing trouble."

"True, Bones. But if they experienced some kind of mechanical problem, the risk might be in leaving them stranded while we take endless readings. It might involve that distorting atmospheric layer. For example, maybe it affected their communicators. That would explain why the first crew was unable to contact the ship, and why the second crew failed to activate the transporter to bring them back.

"They could be starving down there, sitting on their acquired information and waiting for someone to haul them out. We have to find out. They could have survived for six weeks. They might not be able to survive six and a half."

"Still a risk," McCoy objected.

Kirk's reply was matter-of-fact. "That's why we're here, Bones." He rose from his seat. "We'll travel light, gentlemen. Phasers, tricorders, communicators—and you'll take a full medical kit, Doctor."

It took only minutes to gather the necessary paraphernalia; then the three officers met in the Transporter Room. Scott was waiting for them. He would handle the beam-down personally.

"Any new information from Sciences, Mr. Scott?" Kirk inquired as they exited from the elevator lift and crossed to the alcove.

"A little, sir," the chief engineer reported. "Mr. Arex says that the distortion layer has been penetrated sufficiently for sensors to reveal a large variety of life forms on the surface. There are substantial concentrations in the area scheduled for your landing, Captain."

McCoy voiced the thought uppermost in their minds. "Any indication of intelligent life?"

"No, Doctor, none." Experienced hands moved over the controls, adjusting settings, checking energy levels. Playing with a man's molecules was a dangerous business.

"No large clusters of life forms in urban patterns, and no hints of city outlines. No rural patterns indicative of large-scale agriculture."

Kirk nodded. "You've set in the coordinates taken from the survey ship's transporter tape? That's where we want to be put down, Scotty."

"Beggin' your pardon, sir," he countered hesitantly, "but if I beam you down in the same place, you could run into the same trouble . . . and end up the same way. Quiet."

"We'll be expecting exactly that, Scotty," Kirk explained. "At the first sign of anything we can't handle, we'll beam back up. Proceed with transporting."

Scott shook his head, ever the pessimist, and mumbled under his breath. That didn't affect the precision with which he engaged the transporter controls. Triple levers rose, and the three officers dissolved into elsewhere.

Kirk experienced the momentary blackout, the disorientation, and the usual twinge of nausea. Then he materialized in an oven.

A blast of humid, hot air struck him like a sockful of hot mud. That first unexpected blast seemed hotter than it actually was. But while conditions at the set-down point were far from arctic, they were bearable.

After checking his footing he turned and took in their surroundings. They were standing on the bank of a steaming lake—Kirk assumed it was a lake; but it could as easily have been an ocean—he couldn't see land across it. Hot springs gurgled all around them, filling the air with feathery streamers of pure steam.

The thermal activity around them was as intense as in the Waimangu valley on Earth—noisy and nervous. But the ground underfoot was firm and gave every indication of having been so for some time. So Kirk discarded his first thought—that the survey crews might have set down on some unstable area, despite the safeguards inherent in transporter sensors.

"Everyone all right?"

Spock nodded, then McCoy.

"Ten meters either way, though," the doctor pointed out, "and we'd have been boiled alive."

Spock already had his science tricorder out and was taking preliminary environmental readings. He frowned. "Unusual that such a lake, of such·extent, could exist under the planetary conditions prevalent at this latitude. Most unusual."

"Speaking of the unusual, Spock . . . ," Kirk interjected. He was pointing at the surface of the lake directly before them.

A shape was rising from the steaming water. One could read the writhing steam into fantastical forms, but this rapidly growing outline was composed of something considerably more solid than water vapor.

It had a saucer-shaped body, limbs of still unseen design but obvious power, and a short, snakelike neck. A vision of quite adequate ugliness bobbed atop that swaying extension.

Spock nonchalantly turned toward it and readjusted his tricorder to take a biologically rather than geologically oriented reading. He studied the results with undivided attention as they appeared in the tiny read-outs.

"Most intriguing," he finally commented.

"I'm not sure 'intriguing' is the word I'd choose," Kirk said, taking a step backward. "That creature may be able to navigate on land as well as in the water." Certainly the apparition showed no sign of slackening its pace.

"I know it can," an excited McCoy decided nervously, "and I don't need a tricorder to tell me so."

In truth, the alien being appeared to be accelerating as it neared them. Beneath heavily lidded eyes, black pupils stared at them with the single-minded blankness of the primitive carnivore. The interlocking fangs which protruded sicklelike from both jaws parted slightly, revealing an uninviting dark gullet.

"Phasers on stun," Kirk ordered sharply. "Stand ready."

Each man pulled out one of the compact weapons, adjusted the tiny wheel on top, and dropped to one knee. Spock held his phaser in one hand and the still-operating tricorder in the other. Both were aimed with precision.

The monster reached the shoreline, and any question of its ability to navigate a nonaquatic environment was answered as it humped enthusiastically toward them.

"Fire!"

Three bursts traversed the space between the men and the huge monster. The creature halted its seallike advance, faltering. The long neck lowered and swung dazedly from side to side.

A second round stopped the monster as if it had frozen. It sat on the shore, momentarily paralyzed. The nightmarish skull dipped until it scraped the sand.

Then, amazingly, it seemed to shake off the effects of the double phaser blast. Its appetite gave way to a blind desire to escape, however. Turning with surprising agility, it rushed back into the lake and vanished beneath the steaming surface.

"Not a very friendly environment," Kirk observed idly, kicking at the warm earth. "I think the survey crew would have come to a similar conclusion." He turned. "They'd probably try for a friendlier area inland. Let's move."

Picking their way cautiously between pools of bubbling clear water and thick, candylike mud, they started away from the water's edge. Once, Kirk knelt to probe the ground with a finger, and pulled it away speedily. The soil here was painfully hot just beneath the surface, but it was stable.

"What do you think, Mr. Spock?" he asked, referring to their first encounter with a representative of Lactran life.

"An interesting and no doubt dangerous animal, Captain," the first officer replied easily, "but not particularly so, and clearly not invulnerable. Certainly not to the kind of weaponry a survey crew has available as standard equipment.

"Nor is it the sort of beast one would expect to catch experienced personnel off-guard. Such teams regularly expect far more lethal attacks. For it to have surprised and rapidly killed not one but two such teams—no, Captain, I think it extremely unlikely."

"Exactly my opinion, Spock." They topped a modest rise and started down the other side. "In such a situation—"

He cut off in mid-sentence, staring in surprise at the land before them.

No steam rose there. There wasn't a hint of a boiling pool or steaming mud pit. The panorama before them was flat, hot—and dry. Only a few isolated outcroppings of weathered rock broke the gravel-and-sand plain. Here and there an occasional patch of defiant green stood out like a flag. The change was startling.

"Desert," muttered McCoy. "Not a very welcome sight either, gentlemen."

Kirk frowned as he pulled out his communicator. "We're on a hill here. Let's see if we can pick up anything on the emergency ground bands." He flipped open the communicator and made the requisite adjustments, then addressed it slowly and distinctly.

"This is Captain James Kirk of the U.S.S. *Enter-*

prise, commanding a Federation rescue party, calling the crew of the survey scout ship *Ariel.* Come in please, come in."

A faint whisper of wind on tired rock, nothing more.

"Try again, Jim," McCoy prompted.

"Captain James Kirk of the Federation cruiser *Enterprise* calling Lieutenant Commander Markel or any members of the Federation survey ship *Ariel.* Are you receiving me? Please acknowledge."

Still silence. Resignedly, he made a slight, standard readjustment on the receiver dial—and was rewarded with a surprise. A slow, steady beep began to sound.

McCoy was startled. "Be damned . . . they're answering!"

The beep continued for several seconds before stopping suddenly. But not before Kirk, who had been frantically adjusting further controls, registered an expression of satisfaction.

"You got a fix on it, Jim."

The captain nodded. "Barely. The signal didn't last very long, and I don't like the way it cut off like that, in the middle of a series." He turned slightly to their left and pointed. "Over that way."

Picking their way down the slight slope, they started off in the indicated direction. "Likely they're close by, staying near the touchdown point like they're supposed to," Kirk murmured tautly. He squinted at the sky. "We'll try this until the heat begins to tell, then have Scotty beam us up for a rest. We can set down and continue on after a break."

"Don't you think it's strange we didn't get a voice reply to your call, Jim?" wondered a puzzled McCoy.

Kirk shrugged. "Could be any number of reasons we didn't. Mechanical trouble with the communicators, as we originally postulated, Bones."

"Never mind counting them, Spock," broke in McCoy dryly, seeing the first officer about to comment. They continued on across the sand in silence, searching for indications of human passage. There were none— no footprints, no trail of shredded tunic, no lost instruments or survival equipment. Nothing but harsh sky, sand, gravel, and heat that stayed just the human side of oppressive.

Nothing moved on that brown-and-yellow landscape. There was no soothing wind to ruffle the compact, squat green growths which leaned possessively to any hint of shade or depression in the ground.

Kirk spent no time studying them. A single casual glance was enough to show there was nothing remarkable about the largest, nothing distinctive about the smallest. It was the fate of six humans that absorbed his thoughts now, not new outposts of alien ecology.

Eventually they reached the other side of the gentle basin they had been crossing and mounted the symmetrical curve of a large dune. Their descent on its opposite side was as fast and awkward as the climb had been slow and controlled. They reached the sandy base and found themselves confronted by another basin, which terminated in a twin of the dune they had just crossed.

"At least it's not thermal springs and hot mud," McCoy observed.

There was a sound like frying fat, and a sheet of flame interdicted their progress. It missed Kirk, who was in the forefront of the little party, by a few saving meters. He scrambled backward.

Slightly to one side of their intended route the gritty yellow-and-brown soil erupted. Sand streamed from crevices and cracks, and a nightmarish skull fringed with spines, its skin decorated like a Gothic cathedral, burst from the ground and turned warty jaws toward them.

"Left . . . run!" Spock yelled, barely in time.

The rippling mouth opened and belched a second stream of fire. It scorched the sand where they had been standing only seconds before.

Stumbling backward even as they pulled their phasers, they found themselves backed against the steep inward side of the dune. All three weapons fired, aimed to strike the monster in that cavernous mouth. The monster paused, then swung ponderous jaws to face them again.

"The lining inside the mouth of a creature that can spit fire," Spock lectured hurriedly, "would seem to be composed of organic material highly resistant to—"

Without knowing what prompted the thought, Kirk yelled, "Aim for the underside of the neck!"

Once more three beams of intense energy crossed the space between the men and their assailant. All three struck the creature in the area between the lower jaw and forelegs.

Once again the effort seemed futile. Instead of trying to incinerate them this time, the monster lunged forward, jaws agape. It was slow, however, and clumsy. The little group scattered. The primitive machinery of its mind turning slowly, the monster singled out one victim—Kirk. It turned toward him, then rose suddenly on thick hind legs.

Broad spadelike claws on its forelegs reached inward, clawing confusedly at its throat. Then it toppled like a leathery gray iceberg to lie unmoving in the yellow sands.

The impact of the monster's fall had thrown Spock to his knees. Now he glanced around in concern as he slowly got to his feet.

"Captain?"

"Here, Spock," came the reply from nearby. "Are you all right?"

"I am undamaged."

Kirk joined him, brushing the sand from his tunic. "Where's Dr. McCoy?" He looked around, suddenly conscious of the fact that the doctor was nowhere to be seen. "Bones . . . Bones!"

A distant, faintly desperate reply sounded. "I'm . . . *mmpggh!*"

Kirk and Spock turned, looking for the source of that brief cry. There was no sign of Dr. McCoy. Then it sounded again, muffled to the point of unintelligibility.

Worriedly, Kirk glanced to his left, then gestured. "I'm not sure. I think the sound came from back there."

They moved slowly down the length of the unconscious creature's massive body. Spock was the first to notice the two spinelike forms protruding from beneath the thick tail.

"Hang on, Bones," Kirk shouted, "we'll get you out!" The officers moved alongside the two projections, which proceeded to twitch insistently. They shoved, but to no avail. "Again, Spock!"

A second effort, both men straining and heaving, failed to move that limp, incredibly solid bulk. And the shifting sand provided poor footing.

"It would seem," a panting Spock ventured, "that another solution is called for, Captain. We cannot lift the tail. Therefore, we must move the doctor."

Kirk eyed him uncertainly, then nodded in understanding. They dropped to their knees and began digging sand with the speed and efficiency of a pair of small mechanical shovels. The thrashing of the doctor's legs added desperation to their efforts, growing more and more frantic with each passing second.

Finally a lower torso and then a pair of arms became visible. Pulling and additional digging brought the rest of the ship's chief physician into the open once more.

McCoy drew his knees against his chest and locked his arms around them, taking long breaths and digging sand from his eyes, nose, and ears.

Spock and Kirk waited and watched worriedly, until McCoy acknowledged the concern in their eyes. "I'm okay, thanks, but the air was just about gone under there." He glanced back at the sloping pit now leading under the tail. "The flesh was slightly humped above me. I had a small air pocket. Smelly, but I wouldn't have traded it for a bottle of the Federation's finest perfume."

"You're sure you're not hurt?" Kirk pressed.

"No . . . just surprised. I didn't even see the tail falling. It isn't every day a dinosaur falls on you." He sneezed and rubbed his sand-scoured nostrils. "If the ground hereabouts had been hard, I'd be just a smear now. But the sand was deep enough, and soft enough, and I was hit just right for the impact to bury me instead of smash me. I lost a little wind, that's all."

Kirk helped McCoy to his feet, then brushed sand from his hands as he turned his gaze beyond the motionless tail. "How much additional desert do you think we'll have to cross, Mr. Spock?"

The first officer checked his tricorder and pointed in the direction the terse signal had come from. "I have no way of judging for certain, Captain, but, extrapolating from temperature and atmospheric readings, at least several additional kilometers. It could be hundreds."

"No," Kirk objected. "The signal wasn't that strong. But we'd better pick up our pace, regardless. There's no cover here, either from the sun, or from any of the other hungry locals. I'd like to make a bit more progress along the signal track before Scotty beams us aboard for a rest period."

They resumed their march across the sands, detouring around the still-stunned mountain which had almost trapped McCoy. But as soon as they resumed walking, Spock lapsed into an introspective silence which Kirk recognized immediately. Something was troubling the first officer. If Spock had something on his mind, something not yet sorted out, he would inform them about it in his own good time.

His own good time came several dozen meters farther into the dry basin. "You know, Captain," he suddenly murmured, "it was unusual the way I seemed to know, rather than guess, that our phasers would be ineffectual while aimed down the carnivore's throat. The creature itself . . . did it not seem familiar to you?"

Kirk thought a moment, and found, to his surprise, that he didn't have to search his memory for very long. The familiarity of the monster had bothered him all along, but it took Spock's query to crystallize it.

"Of course . . . I've seen soloids of something just like it on Canopus Three. That's impossible, though. Canopus is many too many parsecs from here." He squinted into the unyielding sunlight.

"True, this desert is very similar to those found on

Canopus Three." His voice faded. "Very similar. In fact, those isolated growths, the color of the petrographic outcrops—they're all remarkably alike."

"Are you suggesting, Captain, that a similar environment presupposes identical evolution?"

"My shoes," McCoy broke in, with undisguised distaste, "are full of sand."

Spock's concentration was broken. "Doctor, your lack of scientific interest is a constant astonishment to me."

"I'll be glad to discuss that with you, Spock, the next time you drop into Sick Bay for some medication, or a checkup."

"No need to become belligerent, Doctor. That was merely a simple observation."

"Spock, your simple observations," McCoy rasped as they trudged toward the top of the next dune, "tend to get on my . . ."

He stopped in mid-sentence, mid-thought, to gape at the scene before them. And he was not alone. Spock and Kirk had also come to a momentary mental halt.

Spread out at the base of the dune was a wall of green so lush and colorful in comparison to the dull plain they had just crossed that it was almost painful to look at.

Clusters of thorn-laden trees and broad, thick bushes interwove with taller emergents and exotically contoured growths drooping with strange fruits. Practically at their feet a stream emerged, vanishing in a sharp curve back into the thriving jungle.

There were distant hints of moss and fern forest, of swamp and tropical lowland. They could almost feel the humidity, smell the rankness of rotting vegetation.

For all that, it looked a lot friendlier than the country they had just traversed. "Food and water—anyone would have a better chance of surviving in there than on that frying pan we just crossed" was McCoy's opinion.

Spock wasn't as sure. Turning slowly, he studied the terrain behind them. His gaze lifted to the far dune. Beyond it, he knew, lay a violently active thermal region bordering a vast, steaming lake.

Again he directed his attention to the riotous landscape before them, listened thoughtfully to the soft susurration of small living things picking their cautious way through the undergrowth.

"Does it not strike you as peculiar, Captain, that two—possibly three—radically different ecologies exist literally side by side? Steaming, unstable shoreline, backed by a thin line of desert, and now another extreme change of climate and living things."

"I've seen stranger sights in my travels, Mr. Spock. What are you driving at?"

"Nothing yet, Captain. Simply another observation." His voice trailed off as he glared at the rain forest beneath the dune, taking this perversion of natural law as a personal affront.

Kirk flipped open his communicator again. "I don't plan to do much walking through *that*—not without extra equipment." He directed his words to the tiny pickup.

"Landing party to *Enterprise*." There was a brief pause, rife with static and interference. But the special tight-beam broadcast Scott employed penetrated the mysterious distortion layer in the atmosphere. Kirk heard the chief engineer's reply clearly.

"Enterprise, Scott here."

"Any new information, Scotty? We're a little puzzled by what we've found down here."

"We've got plenty of confusing readings here, too, Captain," Scott confessed. "There appears to be a large concentration of life forms slightly less than a hundred kilometers north-northeast of your present position. How large we can't tell—this blasted distortion effect jumbles every sensor reading we get. I'm informed that it *could* be a city . . . or just a central gathering place for migratory animals. I said our readings were inconclusive.

"That's all so far. Lieutenant Arex is supervising information resolution. He hopes to have a more specific analysis of the data within an hour."

"Very good, Scotty." He muttered to himself, "Northeast." Then, louder, "That's the direction of the signal we received, Mr. Scott."

"I could transport you to the region of life-form concentration, Captain."

"Negative to that, Scotty. We don't know that the missing crew is part of that concentration. They could be anywhere in between, and we can't risk skipping over them. We'll have to do this kilometer by kilometer. Let us know the moment Mr. Arex comes up with a determination of that reading, though. We'll continue in the plotted direction for a while longer. Kirk out."

"Aye, Captain. Engineering out."

Kirk put the communicator away as they carefully picked their way down the dune. They paused at the edge of the jungle, fascinated by the way the rich flora appeared to spring with supernal suddenness from the periphery of bone-dry desert.

"I don't like it, Jim," McCoy finally ventured. "Too many unlikelihoods here. Why only the one short signal? You can argue all you want, but to me that implies something other than mechanical failure."

"I'm not ruling out anything, Bones," Kirk replied slowly. "Their inability to respond further could be due to something we can't imagine. It does prove that at least one member of the survey team is still alive, though. Alive and alert enough to be monitoring an unexpected query."

"Apparently alive, Captain," Spock amended. "The signal could have been sent by other than human hands."

"There's no profit in pessimism, Mr. Spock. For the moment I choose to believe they are alive."

They reached the edge of the stream. McCoy glanced at it briefly before kneeling to satisfy the thirst that had built up in him during the desert crossing.

His hands had barely broken the surface of the water when Spock put a restraining hand on his shoulder. The doctor looked up, puzzled, to see Spock staring at the pool.

"Allow me to test the water first, Dr. McCoy."

McCoy eyed the first officer dubiously, then turned his gaze downward again and stirred the water with a finger. He shrugged. "Go ahead, Spock, but I've analyzed enough water to know a drinkable stream when I see one. You know that, too."

"Nevertheless," Spock insisted. The readjusted tricorder was played over the surface of the rippling brook. Spock concluded the brief survey and studied the subsequent readouts, sending semaphore signals with his eyebrows.

"Well?" an irritated McCoy finally pressed.

"As you surmised, Doctor, the water is certainly drinkable."

McCoy looked satisfied, if still irritated, and bent again to drink.

"However, that is not what prompted my uncertainty," Spock concluded. McCoy looked up at him. "Captain, this water is *too* pure."

McCoy grimaced and scooped up a double handful. He downed it, sipped a second and third, concluding by wiping his parched face with wet hands.

"It tastes just fine to me, Spock."

"Despite that, it is too pure, Doctor," Spock insisted emphatically. "Consider what that means."

Kirk chose his words carefully. "Then what you're saying, Spock, is that it's too good to be true?"

"I would say that evaluation is decidedly understated, Captain." Spock studied the silent wall of green as if it might disgorge a hostile alien horde at any moment.

"Water of this purity flowing freely through thick vegetation growing on loose, loamy soil is not only unnatural, it is positively illogical. As illogical"—and he made a sweeping gesture with one arm—"as the proximity of such a rain forest as this to the desert we just crossed." He knelt and scooped up a handful of dirt.

"Note the composition and consistency of the ground we are standing on now." He sifted it through his fingers. "Fine sand and well-worn gravel of feldspar, quartz, and mica." He stood and dropped the dirt. "It barely supports a few stunted shrubs."

He took two steps forward. "Suddenly, I am in a region of climactic floral development, standing on soil"—and he kicked at the thick soil—"of self-evident fecundity."

"I'm not sure I follow you, Spock," the captain commented.

His first officer gestured all around. "Don't you see it, Captain, Dr. McCoy? It's the abruptness. There is no blending of jungle into desert, desert into jungle, or desert into thermal lowland. The borders between widely divergent ecologies are as sharp as if they had been drawn with a knife."

"Which means what?" wondered McCoy.

Spock drew himself up, then spoke slowly. "It is my theory that what we have seen and encountered since we've landed has been carefully manufactured and not naturally evolved. Environmental manipulation on a large scale has taken place here."

"Terraforming," McCoy muttered. "Or Vulcanforming, or whatever . . . I see. A process which implies the presence of highly intelligent life forms." Suddenly he found himself staring at the green ramparts with nervous expectancy.

Kirk rubbed at his dry chin. "Reasonable as far as it goes, Mr. Spock. But Terraforming usually follows a consistent pattern." He kicked at the ground, sending yellow sand to stain the dark earth of the forest. "On the strength of your own observations, this hardly seems consistent."

"It does appear to be almost random choice, Captain. Unless, of course, the randomness *is* the pattern."

McCoy sighed resignedly. "Spock, don't you ever say anything straight out?"

Spock turned a blank stare on him. "I thought I just did, Doctor."

"Gentlemen, please," Kirk pleaded, "not now. We have work to do."

A short march parallel to the lush greenery brought them to a path that charged in lazy curves deep into the forest. It might have been worn by the passage of many jungle dwellers . . . or it might have been cut. It was another piece of a puzzle that seemed to be growing more and more complex.

The jungle itself bore one similarity to the desert region they'd crossed—its familiarity. Like the Canopus III desert analog, this jungle possessed an almost recognizable pattern which Kirk struggled to place in his mental catalog of well-known alien environments. But identification of the forest world in question remained just beyond his thoughts.

Kirk studied the fibrous exterior of the large tree ferns they were now passing between. Those striking purple-and-puce convolutions were familiar from a well-studied text. To find the environment of one planet reproduced here was startling enough. To find two in such close proximity to each other held profound implications.

"Spock," he began easily, "what do you think of—"

A violent warning cough sounded in front of them. It was followed by a hoarse roar. One, two, three forms and more appeared on the open trail ahead. The powerful spotted bodies showed bristling dark fur and deep-set, angry eyes.

The pack of doglike creatures remained frozen, obviously startled by the appearance of the three figures. They sported huge curved claws more suited to some clumsy digging creature like a sloth, and long thin fangs. Insectoid antennae projected from the thick ridges of thrusting bone above the eyes.

Those eyes narrowed now, with all the expectancy of an archeologist coming upon the bust of an emperor instead of yet another pottery shard. Visual evidence of unfriendly intentions seeped from thick-lipped muzzles. The pack began to edge toward the intruders.

With corresponding caution and patience the three men started retreating.

"There was a cave in that cliff face we just passed," Kirk whispered. "It didn't look too dcep—but it's bound to be better than standing here in the open. If we can make it . . ."

They picked up their pace slightly, still facing the

approaching pack. But, whether through impatience, hunger, or divination of Kirk's intentions, the pack leaders abruptly charged.

"You two, run for it!" Kirk shouted, pulling his phaser and dropping to one knee. "I'll hold them off. They can outflank us all here."

"May I suggest. Captain, that three phasers—"

"Get moving, Mr. Spock!" The first officer hesitated, then turned and ran with McCoy for the cave. His phaser still set to stun, Kirk fired at the nearest of the loathsome apparitions. It yelped once before folding up on the ground.

That was the signal for the rest of the pack to split up. Sinister rustlings and cracklings began to sound on both sides. Kirk fired again, dropping one lean shape that showed against the green on his right. He couldn't hope to get them all—they would come too often from too many directions.

He saw movement out of the corner of an eye and whirled to find Spock and McCoy racing back toward him.

"I thought I told you two to set up your defense in the cave!" he said angrily.

Spock's phaser beam shot past him to knock the legs out from under one of the creatures that had crawled to within jumping distance of the captain. The animal quivered and was still.

"There is a small problem," he explained smoothly.

"A large problem," corrected McCoy, turning to point back the way they had come and simultaneously firing at a low shape.

With Spock and the doctor covering, Kirk was able to divert his attention long enough to peer back down the path through the jungle. From here the cave entrance was barely visible, a dark shadow beneath the looming, fern-studded cliff.

Something was coming out of that cave.

It slid sinuously along the soft soil, emerging from the recesses of the cave like a worm from an apple. It was massive, reptilian, and two-headed. Further description called for extreme adjectives Kirk had no time to dwell on.

"Stay together—and keep backing up toward it," he ordered tightly.

"Jim . . . !" McCoy started to protest.

"No time to argue, Bones—do it!"

McCoy looked anxious but took up a position alongside the captain. Spock was already firing from his other side. As the pack started to emerge from the forest, the officers kept retreating toward the cave—and toward the horror that was coming out to meet them . . .

II

It reached the point where McCoy decided he would rather turn his phaser on himself. "Jim . . . we can't keep . . ."

He didn't even have time to argue any more, so tight had the pack closed in. Not only that, but it turned out that the resistance of the doglike creatures to the phaser beams was considerable. The beams knocked them out, but those first stunned were back on their feet again and once more closing in for the kill.

"When I yell," Kirk ordered, "cut your phasers and dive for that thick copse over there."

McCoy looked in the indicated direction, but saw only a large clump of high grass too thin to keep out a determined mouse, much less a mass of bloodthirsty beasts.

And Spock nodded, apparently concurring in this madness!

The pack was nearly on them now. It had become so bad that McCoy almost beamed Kirk in taking one of the monsters before it could sink scimitarlike fangs into the captain's right shoulder.

At that point, Kirk shouted, *"Now!"* and plunged headfirst toward the high brush. Spock sprayed the pack with a last sustained burst of phaser fire and joined him. Both were a step behind McCoy.

The pack leaders sprang ahead. That concerted action drew the undivided attention of the oncoming leviathan. Its foremost segments expanded. The driving head opened to seize the nearest pack member in one set of jaws.

The quasi-canine screamed, twisted, snapping uselessly at the armored skull. Its fellows, their memories extending only to the immediate prey, forgot their smaller quarry to attack the flanks of the snake-thing.

Two sets of long fangs cut and stabbed at the iridescent yellow and green body. Pained, the Janussnake twitched convulsively, pure muscle sending the two attackers flying into oblivion among the surrounding trees.

Less-bloodied eyes watched from the safety of the neutral grass.

"Stay low and slow," Kirk urged his companions, "and let's edge around behind this."

Nothing challenged them, and they reached the head of the path, the point where the pack had emerged, without incident. They kept to the bordering brush for another thousand meters, though, despite the fact that the pack's attention was occupied elsewhere. Like all creatures of limited intelligence, the dog-beasts' span of attention was brief and easily diverted. There was no point in drawing unnecessary attention to their retreat.

Behind them, the monster reptile snapped and coiled about the harrying pack . . . a colossus assailed by hornets.

"I begin to understand the difficulties even an experienced survey team might encounter here." Spock breathed evenly as they jogged down the path, now well away from the bloody clearing.

"I don't see how anyone could survive on the surface of this world for six weeks, cut off from a base ship and outside support," puffed McCoy.

Kirk observed sharply, "Don't prejudge them, Bones—we're still alive, aren't we?"

"That's true, Captain," Spock observed, slowing, his gaze focused on something high up and ahead of them. "However, it is arguable if this can be called surviving." He gestured at the cause of his comment.

"I wonder if hunting is merely bad hereabouts, or if we constitute some sort of edible novelty to the local fauna."

Through the gap in the trees ahead, Kirk could see three narrow-bodied winged horrors heading straight at them in a long, gliding dive. They shared some of the characteristics of both the pack and the two-headed snake-thing. They had reptilian snouts and scaly wings, but the lithe bodies were coated with fur, and they didn't have the cold eyes of the unblinking reptile.

"Keep your phasers on stun, but be prepared to shift to a stronger beam if necessary," ordered Kirk—rather tiredly, McCoy thought.

McCoy was right. Kirk had had about enough of this world's unrelenting attacks. In light of the steady assault, the Federation edicts forbidding the avoidable destruction of alien life were beginning to grate a bit.

Once more the three officers assumed firing position, once again triple poles of light crossed open air. And the winged dragon-shapes continued their confident dive right toward them.

"Useless!" yelped McCoy, his fingers moving to adjust the setting on his weapon.

"Steady, Bones," urged Kirk. "These are just like the dargoneers on Maraville—the stun charge will get to them eventually."

"Before they get to us?" McCoy murmured, his finger moving back from the setting wheel. He held down the trigger of his phaser, as the flying reptiles continued to come nearer and nearer.

Then a most peculiar thing happened.

The dargoneers jerked up in midair, their heads snapping up and back and their wings abruptly beating unsteadily at the air. Ignoring the continued beaming, they seemed to get control of themselves one by one, turned, and flew off in separate directions.

With nothing left to beam, McCoy clicked off his phaser. Lower jaw hanging open, he stared at the spot in the sky where the seemingly unstoppable aerial meat-eaters had come up short.

"Now that," he observed bemusedly, "is more than passing strange."

"An invisible force field, Doctor," Spock observed. "The knife I was talking about before." He turned to look at Kirk. "I think if we attempt to return the way we've come, Captain, we will find similar fields separating the three environments we have thus far encountered. They were absent when we landed but have apparently been restored."

"Plausible enough, Spock," replied a worried Kirk. "But why shut down such fields in the first place?"

"I cannot imagine, Captain. To find out, I believe we must locate those who have created the fields in question, as well as transformed this section of the planet into a multitude of adjoining alien environments."

"That implies—" Kirk began, but something cut off his breath. He had the sensation of being lifted clear off the ground, experienced that peculiar sense of helplessness one has when one's feet no longer have contact with anything solid. It was a common enough experience in free-fall space, but highly disconcerting on solid ground.

He felt something like a metal band fastened around his waist. When he looked down he saw a gray, wide coil tight around his middle. It didn't look like metal. He put both hands against it and shoved.

It didn't feel like metal, either.

Then he turned and looked behind him and saw what had picked him up as neatly as an elephant plucks a lone peanut. He was in the grasp of the tail end—he supposed it could as easily be the front end—of a creature some six or seven meters in length. It was built low to the ground and had no visible external features. No eyes, mouth, head, arms, or legs—nothing save this single flexible tail or tentacle.

It looked very much like a common garden slug, yet it wasn't ugly. The aura of intelligence, of purposeful, controlled power that Kirk sensed, removed any twinge of xenophobia he might have felt at the mere sight of it.

The creature started to move off down a partially concealed path. Kirk tried to observe its method of locomotion and found he couldn't see beneath its slightly horny, skirtlike lower edge. Whether on legs, cilia, horny plates, or something unimaginable, the creature moved smoothly across sometimes uneven terrain.

At the moment Kirk was more interested in the front end of the creature, for he had to assume it was traveling headfirst. That end showed a single tubular mouth that seemed to study him at length before turning back ahead. Although unable to slip free, he discovered he could turn his upper body easily enough. Looking back, he saw McCoy and Spock following, each similarly pinioned in the grip of one of the dull-hued creatures.

The limb that held him terminated in several smaller divisions, which were in turn separated into still smaller wiggling filaments. The flexibility of those digits was promptly demonstrated when he tried to reach his phaser. One curled around it and plucked it from his waist.

He managed to pull his communicator clear, but that surprisingly delicate organ circled another part of itself around the compact instrument and tugged it firmly from his hand. The action was irresistible without being crudely violent. Whatever had control of him, then, was interested in keeping him intact and reasonably healthy.

That knowledge, along with the fact that no attempt was made to draw him closer to that strange tubed mouth, enabled Kirk to relax ever so slightly.

As soon as the path opened into a cleared, well-kept trail, the three slugs accelerated astonishingly. Their lower limbs might be hidden, but they were amazingly efficient. And despite the speed, the tail-tentacle held Kirk firmly enough so that the ride was not as bumpy as he had feared.

"Would ... would you say this is an intelligent life form, Mr. Spock?" he called long minutes later, his initial evaluation of their captors complete.

"It is difficult to say for certain at this time, Captain," Spock called from behind. "Thus far their only action that could be construed as intelligently formulated was the removal of our phasers and communicators. That could be an acquired or taught action, however. They may be more than advanced domestic animals."

As Kirk considered this, he noticed the squarish shape still slung over the first officer's shoulder. "Intelligent or not, they forgot something, Spock. Can you get at your tricorder?"

"I think so, Captain." One arm was pinned firmly to his side, but he still managed to work the other around enough to fumble at the compact instrument's controls. It was hard to adjust the sensors with only one hand. If he could retain control long enough to take even a few preliminary readings, it might tell them a great deal about—

Two protrusions of the multilimbed tail plucked the tricorder neatly from his shoulder.

"I believe I have an answer, Captain, to the basic question. If these are merely trained animals, their attention span and selectivity are extraordinary. Consequently, even if they are not the masters of this world, I think it reasonable to say they can be considered intelligent on their own."

"Personally I could do with a few more answers than that," a discouraged, aching McCoy called from the back of the strange column. "We've been traveling like this for what feels like hours. Where are they taking us?"

"As near as I can tell, Bones, we're moving northeast, in the approximate direction of that life-form concentration Mr. Scott reported on." His expression turned wry. "It would be a help if he had clarified just what that concentration is, and could let us know. We'd have some idea of what we're heading into."

"I think it more likely, Captain, that we will be able to identify it for Mr. Scott." He gestured with his free hand. "Look ahead."

Kirk turned his attention forward again. They were just coming to the crest of a hill, and he had a glimpse of something distant and pale through the green mesh.

Then they were over the steep slope and traveling down on the opposite side, their peculiar captors never slackening the pace.

The city spread out before them, marching in neat ranks of low, blocklike buildings to the distant horizon. It was an urban complex laid out close to the ground, rather than high and skyward as many of the great Federation centers were. The only interruptions in the field of gently rounded structures were provided by glistening bodies of water, pools, and streams—and by an alien-conceived yet still attractive landscaping. It was not a place Kirk would have liked to live in, but that didn't prevent him from admiring its unmistakable, utilitarian beauty.

"Quite a metropolis," he finally murmured. Spock concurred fully.

"If these are the builders and not servants, they are capable of admirable feats of construction."

"I'm thrilled you two can admire the local talent," McCoy commented sardonically, "but I still have this sick feeling that we're about to become someone's lunch."

Spock looked indifferently confident. "For a creature of this size, Doctor, you would hardly be more than an appetizer."

"Now there's a comforting thought!" McCoy snorted. "Not only am I going to be eaten, but even my passing'll rate hardly a burp."

"We're slowing down," Kirk noticed.

They had come up against the base of yet another hill. Since it was no steeper than the one they had just crossed, Kirk wondered at the stop. Then he noticed that the creature holding Spock had moved to the hill-face and was doing something to a section of the ground.

His guess was confirmed as the reason for their halt became obvious. There was a muted hum from somewhere ahead as the hillside, complete with vegetation and rocky outcroppings, began to slide upward into a concealed recess.

Behind it a large, well-lit cavern appeared, dominated by a huge, silvery cylindrical form which threw back the morning sun in a way only highly machined metal can.

They started forward again. When they neared the cylinder, Kirk thought it was suspended freely in midair. As they moved closer, though, he could see dust motes floating in the air around the base of the metal construct. It was riding on a cushion of air—or something more advanced and less identifiable.

They entered the cylinder through an oval opening in its side. Kirk wondered if their captors also traveled on a cushion of air. That would explain the lack of visible limbs. Come to think of it, this cylinder bore some resemblance to the Lactrans' own bodies.

It grew dark as the humming hillside behind them slid back into place, but only for a moment. Some hidden device compensated, and the interior light grew correspondingly brighter. Kirk tried to identify the source of illumination, but without success. The interior of the cylinder showed nothing like a window, fluorescent panel, concealed tube light, or anything else recognizable as a light source. There was only the smooth metal, his companions, and their three enigmatic, silent captors.

"They're undoubtedly taking us to that city," he ventured aloud, as the faintest hint of motion jarred the craft. "If we could manage to communicate with some of their leaders . . ."

"They don't seem very interested in communication with us," McCoy noted curtly, staring down at the dull gray back of his alien. "That's assuming they're capable of interspecies communication at all."

"I'd tend to think like that, too, Bones," agreed

Kirk, "except every now and then I seem to feel something knocking about the inside of my mind, something that won't stay still long enough for me to fix on it. Like daydreaming. When we reach the city—"

He broke off as the oval portal drew aside with unexpected speed. Their hosts slid through the opening, still showing no strain from their bipedal burdens. At no time, Kirk marveled, had they let their load down to rest.

"We're . . . we're already here?" wondered McCoy, staring in all directions. Spock's amazement was still directed at their means of transportation.

"Remarkable. I experienced none of the sensations of traveling at high speed, yet we have obviously been carried at tremendous velocity. I would very much like a look at the mechanisms involved."

Kirk wasn't listening. His gaze was reserved for the big chamber in which they now found themselves. The vaulted room appeared to be divided into doorless compartments dominated by intricate yet massive machinery. Occasionally, complex structures of metal overhead bathed them in intermittent washes of multicolored light.

A short . . . walk, crawl? He couldn't say, but by some means they entered one such side compartment. The powerful tail-hands dipped, and Kirk, Spock, and McCoy found themselves deposited gently on the ground with as much care as they had been picked up.

That was the one comforting aspect of this entire episode so far. Throughout the entire journey and despite their apparent indifference, the slug-creatures had taken pains to avoid even bruising any of their captives. Nor had they made anything resembling an overtly hostile gesture.

"Any ideas, Doctor?"

"Only one, Jim," replied McCoy, studying their uninspiring, pale-walled alcove, "and it's not very appealing. I'd guess they're doing exactly what we would do in a similar set of circumstances."

"Which is?"

"Well," he continued, as Spock knelt to examine the

half-metal, half-porcelain surface they stood on, "if we encountered an alien creature we'd never seen before on a Federation world, one which science records made no mention of, the first thing we'd do is make sure it was free of harmful bacteria, germs, and other assorted little surprises.

"I wouldn't be surprised if those colored beams we passed through had something to do with insuring our hosts' health. That accomplished, we'd next proceed to see if our visitor were intelligent."

"Congratulations, Doctor," Spock said, looking up from his study of the floor. "All most logical assumptions."

"I told you you should drop by the medical lab sometime."

"A more important question, gentlemen," Kirk interrupted, "is whether or not there's a way out of here." He pointed. "As you can see, we've been left alone."

Indeed, there was no sign of their captors. The vast floor of the chamber was deserted.

"Gone off to report our appearance, maybe," Kirk suggested. He started toward the exit and was brought up short by a half-anticipated barrier. The sensation was akin to that of running into a giant sponge.

Reaching out, he slowly tested the apparently normal air before them. It wasn't hard and unyielding as some such barriers were. Instead, he could push into it; but resistance grew stronger and stronger until further progress grew impossible. At that point, exerting additional strength merely caused his probing fingers to slide off in various directions, as though he were pressing on slippery glass.

"Force field, all right," Kirk murmured. "It seems harmless enough. In fact, if it's designed to do anything, it's to keep those inside undamaged if they try to escape. Absorbs impact rather than resisting it bluntly."

"The bars of a cage are just as harmless," McCoy observed pointedly, "unless you're viewing them from the inside. And we are definitely on the inside." He moved up to the force field. "Let's see if this field is impervious to everything." He cupped his hands and shouted.

"Hey, listen, let us out of here . . . we're as curious about you as you are about us, blast it!"

Something tickled his head.

"A wasteful use of energy, Doctor," Spock commented. "I believe they can hear us quite well without your shouting." He eyed them closely. "I received definite hints of thought projections. I understand that humans are not as sensitive, but did either of you experience anything just now?"

Both Kirk and McCoy nodded.

Spock looked satisfied. "I thought I had detected similar impressions earlier, but could not be certain. I am now. Clearly, they are purely telepathic."

Kirk looked puzzled. "We've encountered telepathic races before, Mr. Spock, and had no trouble communicating with them. Why can't we get a grip on any of the local transmissions? I have the feeling I can almost see an image forming in my mind, but it never becomes stronger than 'almost.' "

"Analysis of the impressions I have received thus far, Captain, would appear to indicate that their thoughts move at a rate far beyond our comprehension. We can only grasp at a fleeting image here and there. That fleeting image we barely sense probably represents many complex thoughts elaborated on at length."

"Surely we can communicate with them somehow," Kirk muttered, "even if only through bits and pieces of information."

"I do not know, Captain," a discouraged Spock mused. "The sheer rapidity of their cogitation, the incredible transport system which brought us here, certain aspects of the instrumentation we have already been exposed to—that could be as advanced compared to Federation civilization as we are to a colony of ants. There also remains the possibility that they could communicate with us and are simply not interested."

"Don't they think we've anything to say?" growled McCoy. "If that's so, they're sadly mistaken. I've got plenty to say to them. Their methods of greeting visitors . . ." His voice trailed off.

"Wait a minute . . . what were they doing out among those other creatures? We never did figure out all those environments."

"You will recall, Doctor," reminded Spock, "that we recognized at least two species from vastly different worlds and ecologies, and we landed in yet another ecology altogether. Remember how we felt that the environments we were passing through appeared not only unrelated to one another but to this world?

"A civilization this advanced might enjoy transforming part of their own planet to"—he hesitated over his choice of terms—"more conveniently provide for their specimens."

"Are you trying to say that we beamed down into some kind of local zoo?"

"That is precisely my theory, Doctor."

"Maybe they'll be kind enough to explain," said Kirk, turning to face the alcove barrier. "They're coming back."

None of them could tell whether the three Lactrans approaching them now were the same three that had brought them there. They inched smoothly across the chamber floor, moving easily via a still unseen, unknown method of transportation, concealed beneath rippling skirts of gray flesh.

Stopping just outside the alcove, the three aliens regarded those within in contemplative silence.

"Examining us," Kirk whispered idly.

"Well, I'm sick of it!" McCoy snorted. He moved up to the force field and gestured emphatically at their captors. "Look, we're as smart as you—maybe a little smarter in some areas—and we don't take kindly to being locked up. I think it's about time you—"

One of the colored beams from above abruptly winked off as the nearest of the three Lactrans reached in with its manipulative tail member to neatly lift the startled doctor from between his companions.

III

"Wait a minute," McCoy yelled. "Do you—"

His world suddenly turned upside down, and he caught his breath. The slug was turning him slowly in its grip and he found himself facing the floor.

"Hey!" Not caring one bit for the position he found himself in, McCoy struggled violently, beating with both arms at the encircling coil of rubbery flesh. The Lactran took no notice of either the doctor's physical or verbal barrage and continued to examine him as unaffectedly as McCoy would an experimental animal in his lab.

"We've got to communicate with them!" Kirk said tightly.

"By all means, communicate," McCoy mumbled, in no mood for diplomacy. His resistance had faded to an occasional weak blow directed at the clasping coil. "Tell it I'm getting dizzy."

"Try, Spock," urged Kirk. "If we concentrate on the same thought, try to pool our effort . . . Try to think *at* it, tell it to release McCoy and put him—"

They never got the opportunity to try. Kirk's voice and concurrent thoughts were interrupted as the other two Lactrans reached into the alcove, one lifting Kirk and the other Spock. They started toward the far end of the vast chamber.

A large section of the far wall appeared to be constructed of the same silvery material as the transportation cylinder. They paused before it and waited while it slid upward. That action Kirk was prepared for.

What he was not prepared for was the sight on the other side.

He had expected to enter another chamber. Now he

blinked as he found himself out in open air and bright sunlight once again, moving rapidly forward.

He glanced down. They were traveling on a moving road or sidewalk of some kind. At the moment it was devoid of any other travelers.

Immense buildings slid past on either side of the roadway. All were constructed of simple gently curved squares and rectangles. There wasn't a single straight line to be seen. Perhaps the Lactrans attached no importance to architecture on merely *efficient* principles.

Kirk realized that the buildings were constructed with the same simpleness and lack of external ornamentation as their hosts.

Despite the oversized proportions of the structures they moved through and the smoothness of the moving roadway, Kirk estimated they had traveled a respectable distance when they finally emerged from the intensively developed area into a vast open plain.

The abruptness of the shift was startling. One minute they were passing through the depths of the monstrous city and the next found themselves in open country.

At least, it *looked* like open country.

Their speed increased. Kirk saw that the broad countryside was actually compartmentalized, divided into sometimes radically varying ecologies. For kilometers it seeme they passed nothing but arboreal creatures—some of the fliers were recognizable, some less so, and a few that utilized exotic methods to defy gravity teased Kirk's curiosity in passing.

Moving beyond, they entered a region of broad fields dotted with trees and flowering shrubs. One such section of grassland proved to be inhabited by a small herd of unicorns, as neat and appealing as if they had just stepped from the pages of an illustrated fairy tale.

"So much for mythology," McCoy commented sadly, as they passed a horned stallion nuzzling its mate.

"Using a nonspecies standard of appreciation, I confess I find them strangely attractive" was Spock's only comment.

"Something even more intriguing coming up, gentlemen," Kirk called to them.

They turned their attention forward, to where the moving roadway executed a sharp turn. At the end of the bend was a new habitat at once more familiar and at the same time more alien than anything they had yet encountered. Three small cottages, as perfect as if they had just been transported whole from Earth to Vulcan, were grouped neatly to the right of the roadway. Kirk took in the carefully planned details as their speed slowed.

Each house had its own swimming pool, handball court, and other accouterments. The emphasis, he noted, was on providing plenty of opportunity and equipment for physical exercise. Each complex was set in a well-landscaped garden.

Having thoroughly studied the arrangement, the officers were not at all surprised when they stopped next to it. They found themselves deposited on the grass nearest the roadway.

A gentle nudge from one of those incredibly versatile and powerful tails urged Kirk forward. As he couldn't very well resist, he accepted the prod and took a few steps onto the lawn.

"Better to do what they want—for now, anyway," he murmured to the others. "We'll figure this out, given time." He turned, as did Spock and McCoy.

The three Lactrans rested there, just off the roadway, conveying the unmistakable impression of watching without eyes. Kirk, receiving the vague feeling that he was expected to do something, walked directly toward them, slowly. A couple of steps were sufficient to bring him up against the expected resilience of the invisible field.

"Our cage has been resurrected again, Bones." No reply. He turned. "Bones?"

McCoy was absorbed in a detailed examination of the ground, but he glanced up at Kirk's second query. There was a hint of genuine surprise in his tone.

"This is real grass, Jim. Real Earth-type common

grass. Real soil, too. Though I wouldn't bet on how deep it goes."

"Exactly," agreed Spock from nearby, where he was engaged in cursory study of a rosebush. "This area has been laboriously prepared for human types."

"How's that again, Spock?" McCoy prompted, struggling to classify what looked like an Earth-type weed.

"We are now apparently exhibits in this zoo."

"Zoo? Exhibits?" McCoy straightened, botany temporarily forgotten. "Well, I'm no exhibit."

"Keeper-animal relationships have always been fluid, Bones," observed Kirk, "even on Earth. We have one category for ourselves and one for most other animals. But then there are the primates and the cetaceans. Intelligent behavior is often a question of artificially applied standards. Maybe the dolphins consider us part of *their* zoo. On this world I think we ought to be flattered if they've put us into the latter category. In any case, they've taken the precaution of putting us behind bars."

"Perhaps we can find out something from our fellow specimens," Spock observed. "I do not believe they could erect this elaborate habitat for us in such an incredibly brief period, despite their technology. They are not gods."

"Fellow specimens?" McCoy echoed in confusion. Then he looked in the direction Spock indicated.

A uniformed man and woman were coming toward them from the farthest of the cottages, walking quickly, the excitement plain on their faces.

"Hello!" the man called as they drew close. "I'm Lieutenant Commander Louis Markel. This is our primary biologist, Lieutenant Randy Bryce. We're darned happy to see you, whoever you are."

"James Kirk, captain of the U.S.S. *Enterprise*. My first officer, Mr. Spock, and chief physician, Dr. McCoy."

"Pleasure beyond words, Captain," Bryce said, her voice high, almost birdlike. "We received your communicator call and acknowledged as best we could."

"Which wasn't as thorough as it should have been,"

admonished McCoy, taking in their surroundings with a wave of one arm. "Why didn't you warn us, at least to say you'd encountered intelligent life?"

Bryce looked at once resentful and dejected. "We didn't have time to warn you." She sighed. "Every now and then they'll let us have this or that piece of equipment to play with. We can use it, under their special supervision, of course. Our hosts may look clumsy, but they can move with astonishing speed when they want to.

"We're kept under constant mental supervision. There may not be any of them in sight, but you can't escape the feeling of being studied. Everything they give us is operational . . . except our phasers, of course. We never know which bit of equipment they'll give us next, or when they'll take it back. When we think we can conceal our true intentions from them, by thinking nonsense thoughts for a while, we work on ways to produce an effective weapon using cannibalized components from scientific equipment—tricorders and so on.

"We were just lucky enough to have a communicator when your call came in, and we decided to answer immediately. We didn't know if you'd be able to receive us again, or how long they'd let us keep the communicator."

"The reason we replied with a directional distress signal instead of with an elaborate warning," Markel put in, "was because we felt a nonverbal communication had a better chance of being ignored." He shook his head. "These creatures are far too perceptive for that. They knew what we were thinking, despite our best efforts to mask our thoughts. Or perhaps our unconcealable excitement worried them, or made them nervous. Anyhow, the communicator was taken away immediately and deactivated."

"You mentioned, Commander, that they provide you with certain items of scientific equipment from time to time," Spock said. "I could certainly use my tricorder."

Markel shook his head and smiled apologetically. "Not a chance, sir. They're kept on a special exhibit table beyond the force wall. We get awfully nervous when a new bunch of patrons or scientists or whatever our visitors are show up and start playing with them. We don't know if we're ever going to see them again in one piece."

Kirk had scanned the cottages earlier from their position by the roadway. Now he lowered his tone as he spoke to Markel.

"There were six of you on the survey roster."

Bryce swallowed and stared at the unattainable blue sky to their left. "We didn't beam down in time to save the others." Kirk eyed her questioningly, and she shook her head in response to his unasked question.

"No, we don't think the Lactrans had anything to do with it. They've been too solicitous of our own welfare." She looked up at him. "You've encountered some of the other inhabitants of this zoo?"

Kirk nodded slowly.

"Well, the only reason we're alive and here to talk to you now is because the Lactrans got to us before some of their exhibits did." She shrugged helplessly. "The others weren't as lucky."

"Or unlucky," Markel corrected philosophically, "if you consider our chances of getting out of this place."

"Don't be so pessimistic, Commander," Kirk urged. "Eventually, my people may locate us. Considering the technology we've seen so far, I'm not sure a forcible attempt at rescue would be a wise idea. I'm *hoping* we can find another way out before Engineer Scott becomes impatient with our continued silence."

Markel's expression eloquently indicated how he felt about that possibility.

"There should be one other member of your group, then," commented Spock.

"Oh, Lieutenant Randolph's in the end house," Bryce told them. "She's running a high fever, and we can't seem to bring it down. The Lactrans don't take any notice of our entreaties—shouted, written, or otherwise. I suspect they don't consider her illness severe enough. And while we're well-supplied with food, they give us nothing in the way of medical supplies."

"I'll check her out," McCoy said reassuringly. "It would be ironic if our captors didn't help because they were afraid of wrongly treating a valuable specimen." He looked grim. "Or maybe they're afraid you might try suicide. A quick dose of some medicine could kill you before they could interfere. Has anyone . . . ?"

Bryce looked back at him steadily. "I'd be a liar if I said the thought hadn't crossed my mind."

McCoy nodded, his expression carefully neutral. "Maybe I can at least diagnose what's wrong with her, but I can't do anything else. Not without my medical kit."

Kirk spoke to Markel as Lieutenant Bryce led McCoy toward the house the three survivors had moved into. "What have you learned about the Lactrans, Commander? You've had a lot more time to study them than we have. All we've been able to determine is that they run this zoo, are telepathic, and possess a very high level of technology. How high we've no way of estimating."

Markel looked disappointed. "I'm afraid we haven't learned much we can add to that, sir. It's difficult to study another culture from behind bars. Particularly when you're being studied yourself. We're not fond of the switch. Also, we were captured and brought here at night.

"But we did see enough to know that this zoo"— and he made encompassing motions with both hands—"is so enormous as to be unbelievable. The only boundaries we saw before we were brought to this place were manufactured ones. There's plenty to hint that the majority of the city is built underground."

Spock made a Vulcan sound indicative of surprise.

"That implies a metropolis of truly gargantuan extent, Commander Markel. On what do you base such an assumption?"

"On what we saw before we were brought here, and on the fact that despite these creatures being obviously diurnal, there were many days when we traveled through the city without seeing a single one besides our hosts."

"And I don't see any now," admitted Kirk, looking around. "That means that if we could slip clear of this force field, we'd have a certain amount of freedom and a good chance of regaining our communicators and phasers. That's a considerable 'if,' however. Have you made any attempts to escape?"

Markel made a muffled sound. "Oh sure." He scooped up a handful of pebbles and spoke as he chucked them into the air. They traveled only a short distance before coming up against the force field and dropping vertically to the ground. "A dozen different ways, a few of them bordering on the insane.

"For example, we tried using one of our communicators, when they allowed us one, to cause a disruption in the field. You can imagine how well we did with that one. We tried the inevitable tunnel." He half smiled, but there was bitterness in it. "I suppose we ought to have guessed that wouldn't work when they permitted us to continue. We couldn't very well hide the work.

"The force wall extends as far below the surface as you're willing to dig. Then we all tried going on a hunger strike. All that brought about was a steady change in our meals. There was nothing to indicate that the Lactrans regarded it as anything like a voluntary protest by intelligent beings. We decided to give it up before we actually starved to death." He threw the final pebble, hard. "Nothing worked. I think we were getting a little crazy when we received your broadcast."

"Have you tried to communicate?" wondered Spock.

"Naturally, sir. Constantly, endlessly. We've tried talking to them, writing, thinking at them, rearranging the landscaping—everything. As far as we can tell, the only response we've been able to generate with our combined efforts is an occasional peculiar quivering movement on the front part of their bodies. I'm afraid I'm not much on quiver semantics."

"They seem motionless enough now," Kirk informed them, nodding toward the roadway. "It looks like we've got company again, gentlemen."

They turned to face the near section of field wall. Two Lactrans were approaching with that by now familiar eerie smoothness. They settled themselves opposite the captives and succeeded in conveying the impression of lavishing their undivided eyeless attention on the tiny group of bipeds.

It produced, Kirk decided, a very cold feeling.

Since the Lactrans appeared content to rest and watch, Kirk and the others decided to use the opportunity to study their captors in turn. They strolled over and stood at the edge of the force field.

"They built this sealed environment for us shortly after we were captured," Markel murmured. "Fairly sprang up around us. That was one of the first solid indications we had that they were telepathic." He stared at the nearest alien, striving to penetrate whatever shield blocked the mind contained within that sluglike mass of protoplasm. "None of us was thinking consciously of anything like this layout," the commander continued, "when we were deposited here. Our thoughts were about as far from comfortable cottages and swimming pools as possible."

"That would appear to indicate that they are capable of reaching into one's mind and withdrawing imagery from memory," Spock suggested. Markel nodded agreement.

"I'd think that would also convince them of our intelligence," Kirk mused. "Still, we haven't even defined our own parameters of intelligence. We've no way of imagining what the standards are in Lactran." He glanced at his first officer.

"You mentioned correctly, Spock, that where mental reception is concerned, you as a Vulcan are more sensitive than the rest of us. That goes for thought projection as well. Try. You may have more luck than Commander Markel and the others."

"I will attempt it, Captain, but I am not optimistic."

Standing still and silent, Spock closed his eyes and drifted rapidly into a trancelike state. Kirk and Markel continually shifted their attention from Spock to the two Lactrans near the field.

Without apparent cause, the front ends of both aliens lifted slightly and twisted, puttylike, toward each other. Whether this action was the result of Spock's efforts was something only the first officer himself could answer.

Spock kept up the effort for several long minutes, then slumped, visibly exhausted by the strain.

"There are the same glimmerings of something supernally intelligent, Captain," he reported slowly. "Far different from anything I've ever encountered before. But again, the rapidity with which they process their thoughts defeats me. I cannot break through on their level. It does not help that they seem to be absorbed in conversation with each other. A two-way effort is required."

"I see. And if one directed its thoughts at you, then it wouldn't matter because it could detect our intelligence on its own." He looked disgusted. "I hate cyclic problems." He brightened.

"Perhaps we'll have more success with a technique I'm sure Commander Markel has tried. A combination of Vulcan thought projection and something graphic. Try writing something, Spock, and concentrating at the same time. Navigational computation, perhaps."

Spock nodded. He broke a suitable dead branch from a nearby tree, then located a patch of ground where the grass cover was nearly nonexistent. The formula he scratched in the bare earth was complex enough to indicate mental powers beyond simple random doodling, yet basic enough to be readily recognizable to any creature with a working knowledge of elementary chemistry. At the same time his eyes glazed over, indicating he was striving to project his thoughts at the watching Lactrans.

This time Kirk noticed a slight shaking, a rippling of the gray mantle that lined the front fringe of both aliens. This was accompanied by coordinated, extensive movements of the tail-tentacle.

"You seem to be getting a response," Kirk murmured with repressed excitement.

Spock stirred, his discomfort apparent even through his muddled voice. 'I have . . . have the vague impression that . . . they are laughing at me."

That implied a general conception of what Spock was writing and at the same time contempt—it didn't make sense. It didn't add up.

It was frustrating and infuriating.

"But basic mathematics," Kirk almost shouted, "has been a universal language among every intelligent race the Federation has encountered."

The first officer blinked and left his state of concentration. "That may be the problem, Captain. Our formulations may be too basic, though this equation is far from simple. It is possible that they are so far ahead of us mathematically that my attempt was comparable to a child's futile struggle to make words with letter blocks. Many creatures can scratch out imitative lines analogous to mathematical equations. Talent in mimicry does not imply the power of creative thought."

"Try something else," Kirk ordered irritably.

"Yes, Captain."

Once more the trance of projection, again a new formula etched into the dirt. Kirk anxiously studied the Lactrans for the signs of recognition due their captive's intelligence. That they were paying attention to Spock seemed clear.

There were definite reactions. The quivering increased and spread to other parts of the aliens' bodies. But, wish as he would, Kirk saw no indication of anything like shocked amazement, no sign of an attempt to contact him. Nor was there anything pressing at his mind.

This line of attack was useless. There was no point in tiring his first officer needlessly. "It's no use, Spock, you may as well relax."

Spock tossed the stick away and rubbed with both hands at his forehead and temple, like a runner massaging his thighs after a steeplechase.

"At least we know they are capable of humor," he observed.

Markel was not amused. "We haven't seen anything funny about this so far, Mr. Spock."

Spock replied imperturbably, "Animals in a zoo rarely do."

Kirk broke the rising tension between the two by turning away from the Lactrans and starting toward the occupied cottage.

"Let's join the others. Right now I feel the need for a bit more human company, and a bit less alien." He wasn't sure whether the unbroken, eyeless stares of the Lactrans were making him angry or uneasy, or both.

Letting either emotion overwhelm continued study of their predicament would not bring them closer to a solution, he reminded himself as they entered the house.

The interior was frightening in its cheeriness. Frightening because the creatures that had constructed the wooden chairs, printed the bright wallpaper, were anything but human. Frightening because those paper and chair designs had been drawn unbidden from the minds of unknowing human beings.

A tall, middle-aged woman was lying on the couch beneath the front window. Her expression and pose, even in that naturally relaxed position, hinted at far more than normal exhaustion. Sweat stood out on her forehead like quicksilver on a plastic sheet.

Lieutenant Bryce stood nearby as Dr. McCoy continued his methodical, patient examination—limb by limb, joint by joint, pressing, feeling, laying on hands because of the absence of instruments of metal and plastic and ceramic. While less accurate, however, those hands were equally sensitive.

Bryce turned at their approach, offering a wan smile. "Captain Kirk, Mr. Spock." She gestured at the prone form. "Lieutenant Nancy Randolph, our cartographer and navigator."

Randolph managed a grin and limp handshakes all around, but even that slight effort clearly exhausted her. Kirk waited until McCoy had concluded his extensive examination, then drew him off toward the rear of the room.

"How is she, and what's the matter with her?"

"She's not well, Jim. As to what's affected her, it's almost impossible to make anything like an accurate diagnosis without proper instrumentation." He took a deep breath.

"If I had to guess, though, I'd say she's picked up some kind of malarial-type infection from an insect bite. I can't tell for certain, of course, much less prescribe any kind of corrective treatment beyond applying cold compresses in hopes of keeping the fever from rising. Bryce has been doing that anyway." He grunted. "If she's not improving, at least she's not getting any worse. But her body can fight the infection only so long. I've got to have my medikit, Jim! Guesses make lousy medication."

Kirk nodded, then turned to walk back to the large front window. The better to enable them to see out? he wondered—or to allow visitors to see in? Angrily, he shrugged the thought away.

The pair of Lactrans had not moved from their resting place. They stayed there, squatting and staring at the house, only occasionally turning front ends to face each other. Kirk knew they were conversing as surely as if they had been shouting in Federation English.

"We haven't seen another Lactran since we arrived except these two," he declared. "Is this standard procedure, Commander Markel? Do these two have a function—are they scientists, or what?"

"It's our joint opinion that they're guards, sir," Markel told him. "Or keepers—the terminology depends on your mood of the moment. Sometimes there are three instead of two, but always at least a couple hovering around somewhere, except when large groups of them appear. They're probably there to see we don't damage ourselves, or each other."

McCoy grunted again. "Very thoughtful of them. I suppose we should feel flattered."

"You mentioned regular meals," Kirk went on. "Do they feed you or supply game so you can fend for yourselves?"

Markel shook his head. "They bring us a large case of various edibles once a week. The stuff is funny-looking, but it tastes okay. I think they synthesized our emergency rations." He smiled at a sudden thought. "If

I'd known, we would have beamed down with steak and seafood instead of concentrates."

"How do they get it to you?"

"I'm not certain. We've never been able to tell if they shut the force wall down completely or just at the point where the food is sent in."

"The point?" Kirk perked up. "They always bring it to the same place?"

"Always," Bryce admitted, nodding. "Near the display case."

"Display case . . . what display case?"

"Behind this house," she continued. "Commander Markel mentioned the table our equipment was kept on. It's set up there, outside the force wall. They have all our toys in there, our digging stones and pointed sticks. That's only appropriate, isn't it?" She turned a worried, tired gaze down to the feverish navigator. "It's all part of the main exhibit—us."

"Phasers, communicators, medical supplies, tricorders, and packs—everything we brought down with us," Markel finished.

"That means my medikit should be there, too," McCoy surmised. "We've got to get it back somehow."

"Possibly we can persuade them to give it to us, Captain," Spock suggested. "It is certain that they are aware of the potential of each device. That is shown by their refusal to return the phasers at any time."

"But the medical equipment wouldn't be harmful," McCoy noted. Spock shook his head, once.

"We have already commented on the possibility of voluntary injury to a despondent captive," the first officer commented, ignoring the sensibilities around him in favor of cold reason. "That explains their reluctance to turn such material over to their captives."

"Even at the expense of losing one of those valuable specimens," McCoy snarled, staring helplessly at the recumbent figure of Lieutenant Randolph. His arms were held stiffly at his sides, the hands curled tightly into fists.

"A strong emotional projection, Doctor."

"What of it?" a belligerent McCoy objected.

"Possibly nothing, but continue with it. Reinforce it, concentrate on it to the exclusion of all else."

McCoy started to say something, hesitated, then nodded as understanding of Spock's intention dawned on him. He let the rage and frustration flow freely over him, dwelt masochistically on the image of a twisted, emaciated Randolph writhing on the couch in her death throes. His face contorted and wrinkled, and he fairly vibrated with the tension. McCoy was almost a parody of concentration.

Parody or not, it seemed to have some effect. Spock was staring out the front window as McCoy concentrated. As he watched, one of the two Lactrans abruptly turned and scurried off out of view.

"One of the aliens has just left his companion, Captain," he reported.

"Keep it up, Bones."

"I'm . . . trying, Jim . . ." McCoy's face was a portrait of exaggerated yet honest concern.

"A little bit longer. Give them a chance and we'll see what happens . . ."

They waited. Markel suddenly broke the silence. He was staring out one of the back windows and called excitedly to the others.

"Back here, Captain!"

His concentration broken by the interruption, McCoy turned and left the house through the back door, along with Spock, Markel, and Bryce. They were just in time to see the Lactran who had left, or possibly another one, withdrawing its multiple-ended tail from the force-field boundary. At a corresponding point inside was a pile of exotic but nourishing-looking fruit and vegetables.

"Food—different food, and it's not feeding time," a puzzled Markel observed.

"I think I understand," began Kirk. "They must have sensed Dr. McCoy's projection of want, of need, and interpreted it as a desire for food. The strength of the projection might explain the new offerings. Possibly they feel we require a different diet than you, at least at the beginning of our captivity." He considered the pile of edibles carefully.

"That means that their telepathic sense is less than perfect, or they would have given us the medical supplies. I'm sorry they didn't, but at the same time it would be foolish to say I'm not glad to see a hint or two of imperfection on our captors' part."

"It's nice to have confirmation of that fact, Jim," agreed McCoy tiredly, "but I could have told you that already. And while you might think me a reactionary anthropomorphist, I can also assure you that they're not pretty." He wiped perspiration from his brow. The steady concentration had exhausted him, though in a fashion different from the way such strains affected Spock.

Logic ordered no rest, however, as Spock suggested, "I believe we should all concentrate on the need for Dr. McCoy's medikit, emphasizing our intention to use it only to help preserve one of our members."

Markel shrugged. "Worth a try."

All five of them went silent, some with eyes closed, others staring hard at the slowly retreating Lactran, each using the method which seemed most effective to him.

The subject of this concentration responded with satisfying suddenness. It turned to regard them quietly, then sidled over to the oddly curved display table.

Waivering over the metal, the tail hesitated over several objects before picking up ... the captain's phaser! For a wild moment Kirk thought that one of their weapons might be returned to them. Similar thoughts occurred to several of the others.

Either because of their thoughts or because of the Lactran's own knowledge, the bulky alien immediately put the weapon down. Kirk cursed himself for giving in so childishly to the offensive image his mind must have conjured up. He resumed concentrating twice as hard on McCoy's medikit.

The Lactran's next choice was more assured. It picked up the necessary container. Handling it as delicately as if it were the prize glass sculpture of a master,

STAR TREK LOG EIGHT 51

it moved toward them and set the kit on the lawn behind the house.

Kirk watched the entire procedure intensely, but
there was nothing to indicate any button depressed or
lever moved to deactivate that section of the force
field.

Still, someone somewhere must have done exactly
that. He couldn't believe that the Lactrans possessed
the physiological ability to walk through their own restraining field with impunity.

He mused on the problem while the others made a
run for the precious medikit, lest the alien change its
mind and return to snatch it from them.

"No telling when they'll decide we've had it long
enough," Markel explained as they ran toward it.
"We've been permitted to keep other equipment anywhere from a few hours to a week."

As McCoy anxiously examined the kit and the others crowded around him, Kirk walked on past to study
the section of force wall the Lactran had inserted it
through.

"It's all here—no damage and nothing altered," declared McCoy finally. "They haven't removed any of
the emergency ampules, either."

"Unfortunately, nothing's changed here, either,"
Kirk replied. "The field's back on." He stared outward,
looking longingly at the table laden with phasers and
other equipment, their own as well as that brought by
the survey team.

"So near and yet so far," he murmured sadly.

Behind him, McCoy was heading for the house.
"Have to see to my patient," he muttered in satisfaction. Doctor, patient, and medical supplies—the tripar-
tite components of his Aesculapian universe were once
more complete.

Kirk watched them walk toward the house. He
bestowed a final, concentrated thought on the retreating Lactran, pleading desperately for a simple,
harmless toy—his communicator.

The Lactran ignored him completely.

IV

Meanwhile others were striving to pierce the isolation which had swallowed up the captain, first officer, and chief physician of the *Enterprise*.

"Are you raising anything yet?" an anxious Scott inquired of Lieutenant M'ress. He stood near the communications console and stared at the squiggles and lines which appeared on various read outs, in the hope that one of them might spell out an answer in plain English.

No explanation was forthcoming from those dispassionate, uncaring instruments, plain or otherwise.

"Not a thing, sirr," M'ress replied. She had answered the same query from Scott with the same information every five minutes since she had taken over for Lieutenant Uhura.

Scott responded with the same order. "Keep at it. They're down there somewhere."

Furiously, he turned over the same old possibilities in his mind. It was highly unlikely that all three officers had experienced a simultaneous breakdown of their communicators, regardless of what might have happened to those carried down by the survey crew.

That left three possibilities.

One, they were unable to use their communicators, for what reason Scott couldn't imagine. Two, their communicators had been rendered inoperative by outside forces. Three . . .

He refused to consider Three. As long as he denied the possibility, it could never come about.

Scottish reasoning can be notoriously perverse, and this was one instance in which Scott utilized its roundabout methodology to the fullest. Spock could say that

Scott thought in pretzels all he wanted to ... as long as the absurd first officer was all right.

As long, the *Enterprise*'s chief engineer thought furiously, as he was all right ...

The little knot of humans left McCoy to his doctoring, aware that their presence could only hinder his ministrations. Lieutenant Bryce lingered the longest, but eventually she, too, left the couch and its tired occupant to join the others in gazing out the front window.

Both guards stood, or sat, where one had been moments before. They regarded the inhabitants of the house with identical but featureless stares. The inhabitants stared back with somewhat more animation.

"Let's sum things up, Commander," Kirk started firmly. "Based on everything that's happened to you since you've been trapped on this world, what's your evaluation of the situation?"

Markel considered for a moment and ticked off his observations on the fingers of one hand. "The Lactrans treat us quite well. They want us alive and healthy and are willing to go to some inconvenience to insure that we remain so ... though they do make occasional mistakes—underestimating the severity of Lieutenant Randolph's condition, for example. Most importantly, they want to keep us right where we are."

"A natural reaction for the curators of a zoo," Spock observed drily.

"We've managed to keep from going crazy," continued Markel, "only just. Part of the time we make studious analyses of our guards, trying to discern differences between them ... with little result. The rest of the time we occupy by plotting absurd escape schemes and executing them, and by making observations of this world not connected with our captors. For example, we've worked out a calendar according to the movements of the Lactran sun and moon. It's a close duplicate of our own, which helps us a little. Oh, and every nine days we draw quite a crowd."

"Undoubtedly the local equivalent of a periodic rest time," commented Spock.

Markel was silent for a while as attention was divided between the guards and the couch, where McCoy made steady, assured motions with his hands and paraphernalia. Then he turned a concerned, unwinking gaze on Kirk.

"Sir, do you think there's any chance of getting out?" It wasn't the sort of statement the leader of a survey crew ought to make, but then, Markel didn't feel much like a leader at the moment. He felt like a laboratory rat crouched at the far corner of its cage, regarding a monstrous hand moving inexorably toward it.

"As long as they keep us alive, there's a chance," Kirk replied, properly encouraging. His private thoughts went unvoiced. "Sometimes the strongest force fields can be negated by the simplest procedures. Tonight we'll try to find a frequency commonality using Dr. McCoy's instrumentation, slightly rearranged, of course."

"I'd say there was no commonality, Captain."

"Not very encouraging, Mr. Spock."

"I am not one for fanciful dreams, sir, as you well know," the first officer replied evenly.

"I never met a Vulcan who was." Markel did not look across at Spock.

"I hope," the target of that barb said carefully, "that was meant to connote the value of being a Vulcan."

"I'm sure it was," Kirk said hastily.

Spock was well in control of himself, but Kirk saw that the survey commander was being pushed by Spock's constant coolness. Spock could only be Spock, however, and he continued relentlessly. His mind could not make room for childishly optimistic speculation where no grounds for such existed.

"I think we should face our situation realistically, Captain. We are specimens in a zoo. We have been taken captive by an alien race of unusual technological accomplishments and unpredictable psychology. To them, we are caged for life. These facts, coupled with the Lactrans' undeniable demonstrations of superior intelligence, do not add up to a very convincing set of factors for eventual escape. And, while not very encouraging, Captain, that is my reasoned assessment of our present situation."

"Thank you, Mr. Spock," Kirk replied. "And mine is, let's sleep on it."

Randolph was a new person the following morning, thanks to McCoy's skilled treatment. New, but not her old self, not yet. Her system would need plenty of time and rest to return to normal strength. So she remained on the couch under doctor's orders as the other five officers left the house.

Kirk was the first one out, and he pulled up short, staring around in surprise. The others followed and displayed varied expressions of equal amazement.

"We seem," Spock observed mildly, "to be drawing quite a crowd."

Indeed, where only the presence of two guards had marred the broad horizon the previous day, there now milled a thickly packed throng of Lactrans. The only visible differences between individuals were slight variations in color and somewhat greater ones in size.

"This is that ninth day I mentioned," Markel informed Kirk, unnecessarily.

"I'll be hanged if I'm going to do tricks for them," grumbled McCoy.

"We can move about as we wish, Doctor," agreed Spock, "but we cannot evade their mental vision. I suggest we attempt to ignore them and make ourselves comfortable."

They moved around to the side of the house, Lieutenant Bryce going inside briefly to inform Randolph of what was going on. The recreational section outside boasted a number of comfortable chairs, and it was into these that the members of the trapped group settled themselves.

Bryce returned, indicating the pool and surrounding equipment. "As you can see, they've given us extensive facilities for enjoying ourselves—and for making sure we stay healthy." She snapped out the words. "A very comfortable wheel, only the rats aren't in the mood to climb in and run in place.

"They feed us," she continued as she relaxed into a free-form of orange plastic, "and apparently think this is all we want. To run, eat, sleep, and"—she paused only slightly—"play."

"Exactly what we would expect from the animals we have in our own zoos," Spock commented. His tone was almost approving. Almost.

"Well, I am not an animal," McCoy muttered disconsolately.

"Scientifically speaking, we all are," Kirk reminded him, then turned to each in sequence. "Instead of learning about us, a subject we're pretty familiar with, why don't we follow Commander Markel's suggestion and try to learn something about them."

Markel looked resigned. "I don't see what more there is we can learn, Captain, unless we can either penetrate their minds or convince them of our intelligence."

"Known fact: They are purely telepathic," Kirk began, restating the obvious. "Mr. Spock is, like all Vulcans, peripherally so, but as yet has not been able to make successful contact with them."

"Their intelligence is so different that I can find no common basis for an exchange of information, let alone for complicated visualizations," Spock added.

"Exactly what did you learn yesterday?" Markel wondered.

"That the thoughts and expressions of adults are incomprehensible to a six-year-old infant," the first officer declaimed, "and that the infant's babblings are regarded with equal incomprehension by adults." He did not have to place his companions into one of the two categories.

"I think we're missing something, Spock," the doctor said.

The first officer turned an interested gaze on McCoy. "What do you mean?"

"Well, we're assuming this extraordinary, impenetrable intelligence level is uniform throughout the population. In any civilization there are the gifted, the norm, and the slow." He nodded once toward the smoothly shifting crowd. "Maybe there are less highly developed minds out there today. It's only natural to expect the keepers to be reasonably advanced. That's not necessarily so of those who come to gawk. Try them. At least we'll have the general public's impression of us, if we're lucky."

"A fine suggestion, Doctor." Spock turned his stare outward, concentrating without exerting the maximum effort of the previous day.

"It is only a vague generalization," he finally murmured softly. "I could be completely wrong, but we appear to frighten some of them—at least the smaller ones. Probably juveniles. The others have mixed feelings: Some are indifferent, some curious, a few find us rather ugly." He blinked. "It is a sign of their advanced civilization that none projected any hint of antagonism toward us."

"Okay, the feelings are mutual," McCoy commented without rancor. Changing the subject abruptly, he asked Kirk, "What about those on board, Jim?"

"Scotty's patient, Bones, when he has to be. Left to his own feelings, he'd probably have beamed down yesterday to see what happened. But he's under orders. He'll exhaust every ounce of patience, try everything to regain contact with us without taking offensive action. But eventually, he's going to get worried enough to take action.

"As I said before, the *Enterprise* might not come out on top in a fight with our silent hosts. No, Scotty will hold off. He'll need some proof we're in danger before sending down an armed force—and we're probably safer here than on board the ship, thanks to the concern of the Lactrans."

"We have to do *something*, then," McCoy exploded, "besides rest on our fundaments and juggle the odds of a Federation–Lactran battle . . . with us in the middle."

"I have a suggestion, Captain, when the doctor is finished."

McCoy threw Spock a sour look and mumbled, "I'm finished, Spock, what's your grand solution?"

"Not solution . . . suggestion," Spock corrected efficiently, completely missing McCoy's sarcasm. "Evidently they can pick up our thought patterns if we all concentrate on the same thing. *If* they care to go to the trouble."

"This is the main problem. Believing that we are animals, it is therefore not worth their effort to descend to our level. Who cares what the vermin think?"

"Yes, yes," Kirk agreed rapidly, "we've already proven that by getting them to give us the medical kit. Where do we go from here?"

"I see no reason not to try an idea that has worked once a second time." The others eyed Spock expectantly. "One of us must pretend to be seriously ill. Even more important, the rest of us must *believe* in the falsified illness, so that our true intentions are masked from the Lactrans. The lie must be close to the truth, for us to have a chance. Our captors are perceptive and react quickly. We have to concentrate strongly on the thought that a communicator is vital to the patient's recovery.

"Naturally, we need not specify in our minds exactly *why* a communicator is required, but it is a thought all of us should be able to hold to." He paused, then went on easily, "Surely a return to the *Enterprise* would be one method of seeing to the health of an ill individual."

"Sounds possible, Spock," Kirk finally concurred. "Let's try it. And, visual stimulus being an aid to concentration, let's move back behind the house so that we can look at the communicators while we're concentrating on one."

There were far fewer Lactrans clustered at the rear of the cottage than they had encountered out front. That was only natural, Spock pointed out, since the best view in any zoo was in front of the cage. Possibly their novelty was wearing off, because no rush of Lactrans appeared to gaze at them from the new vantage point.

Only a small number were clustered by the display

table. As they neared the field wall, Kirk saw that one of the smaller aliens was busily engaged in examining the equipment laid out on the table. The larger ones rested nearby, apparently deep in telepathic conversation.

"Okay, who's our candidate for convincing convulsions?" McCoy wondered aloud.

"I'll do it," Kirk said immediately. "I'm sick of this place and sick of our situation, so I won't have to exaggerate too much. The rest of you concentrate like hell on the nearest communicator."

"Maybe we'll get lucky," Markel observed, his attention focused on the display table. "That's a little one pretty much alone with the instruments. If Mr. Spock's right, it could be a youngster."

"Spock wasn't sure, Commander," Kirk reminded him. "It might merely be a small adult. Or maybe the adults are the smaller of the species." Markel looked disappointed.

"Try to think about Captain Kirk's visible manifestations of illness," Spock advised the others, "instead of considering his actual condition. We must strive to project an aura of intense worry and concern, to the exclusion of all other thoughts."

"And remember, we have to be quick," Kirk admonished. "As soon as I get my hands on a communicator, I'll try to get enough information through to whoever answers so that they'll know we require an immediate beam-aboard." He settled himself close to the field wall.

"Ready now . . ."

Kirk became a dervish, spinning, whirling, hopping about, clutching at his head, and finally bending over with both hands pressed to his stomach. He rolled on the ground, bugging his eyes and choking, generally presenting the appearance of a being whose health was somewhat less than ideal.

The others moved to form a half circle around him, leaving the section between Kirk and the force field unblocked. They stared down at the body in spasms, their faces reflecting the agony they forced themselves to feel.

The effect upon the small Lactran studying their equipment was immediate. It turned its front end toward the enclosure and gave that eerie impression of ogling without optics. Moments came and went, while Kirk struggled to maintain the illusion of impending death and Spock wondered if they were wasting their time.

The versatile tail drifted over the exhibit table, finally settling on some of the survey team's emergency medical supplies. Turning sideways, the Lactran extended its tail and deposited the sealed containers inside the field, close to Kirk's thrashing legs.

"It has the idea," Spock murmured, his eyes never straying from Kirk's writhing form. "We must concentrate harder on the necessary remedy. The communicator . . . it is the only thing that will save the captain. The only thing . . . he'll die horribly without it, remember. That's all you can think about, the captain dying . . . unless . . . he gets . . . the communicator . . ."

Several minutes of truly inspired gesticulating on Kirk's part coupled with his companions' shunning of the proffered medical supplies, prompted the Lactran to reach farther into the field cage to nudge the containers closer to the pitiful, suffering specimen.

When this further offering was also ignored, the slug turned back to the exhibits. This time it picked up one of the communicators, the compact device looking even tinier in the grip of that massive gray limb.

But the ruse was only partly successful. Either the Lactran suspected the depth of their need for this particular instrument, or else it was unsure of itself, but, whatever the reason, it decided to keep a close eye on its utilization. So instead of handing over the communicator, it entered the enclosure with it.

Like an elastic crane the tail swooped around and down, to offer the instrument to Kirk. Apparently the Lactrans held to the "heal thyself" principle. Well, Kirk was more than willing to abide by it. He raised a quivering, feeble hand and grasped it, bringing the instrument down toward his mouth. As soon as he had it opened and activated, he underwent a remarkable transition. In fact, his symptoms of advanced disease vanished as though they had never existed.

"Enterprise, Enterprise, this is the captain. Beam us aboard immediately, all of—"

The communicator was torn from his grip before he could finish. Had he not let go, the Lactran would have taken his arm along with the instrument.

Whether it was the physical or mental commotion, or both, something finally caused the two large Lactrans standing nearest the exhibit table to cease their inaudible conversation and whirl. They started toward the force field.

A familiar flickering in the air had commenced behind the force wall, a colorful shimmering that Kirk gaped at in horror. The transporter effect was not engulfing himself, Spock, or any of the other anxious captives.

The smaller Lactran brightened once and was gone.

Scott fought the transporter controls, having reacted instantly to Kirk's shipwide call. He had focused on the area surrounding the exact position of the communicator, as pinpointed by the *Enterprise*'s communications computer.

Readouts indicated he had locked onto a substantial mass—presumably the captain and the rest of the landing party, including any survivors from the *Ariel.*

He stared expectantly at the alcove, where something was beginning to take shape.

"Captain," he began, "for a minute we thought sure . . ." He stared, swallowed. "What in cosmos . . . ?"

Instead of the captain, Mr. Spock, or anyone else, a two-and-a-half-meter-long monstrosity was coalescing in the chamber. It looked like a cross between a cucumber and a squid, combining the least desirable features of both.

Its front end—or was it the back?—moped around rapidly, until it was pointed at Scott. The engineer's hackles rose as he felt as if something unclean were picking at his mind. At the same time the long tail whipped around, secondary limbs contracting.

Scott ducked down behind the console. The tentacle probed. As it did so the *Enterprise*'s chief engineer made like a foot soldier and scuttled fast for the door.

A first palm thrust sent the metal partition sliding shut behind him. A second activated the wall intercom.

"Scott here . . . Security, full team to the Main Transporter Room, on the double! We've—" Metal groaned behind him.

The door had begun to buckle inward. It was still bending when three security guards skidded around the corridor corner, phasers held at the ready.

"I beamed up something out of a bad hangover," Scott yelled at them. "The captain sent an emergency message, and instead of him we got—"

The door gave in with a musical *spannggg,* and Scott's half-coherent explanation went no further.

"Watch it!" he yelled, stumbling backward.

The door slammed down against the deck. Scott thought of yelling for phasers to be set on stun, but changed his mind when he remembered through the confusion of the moment that security phasers were never preset to deliver a lethal charge.

Nor was it necessary to give an order to fire. Faced with an eight-foot-long slug emerging from behind a crumpled door and a wildly gesturing officer, they decided unanimously to try nonverbal means of persuasion on the apparent cause of the trouble.

Three phasers fired, three beams struck the Lactran. Its skin seemed to ripple slightly . . . and that was all. But the creature stopped, though both Scott and the security personnel had a feeling it wasn't because of the phaser attack.

Scott began retreating down the corridor to organize a larger capture party, but immediately came to a jerking halt as though an invisible cable around his head had snapped taut. Both hands went to his suddenly throbbing skull, where tiny gnomes had set up a small warp-engine and were running it at overdrive.

All three guards, being closer to the intense mental blast, had been knocked to the floor. Sliding along the deck like a heavy metal ingot on oil, the invader sprinted forward, swept up Scott with its tail, and raced down the corridor.

Behind, the guards struggled to find their phasers, their composure, and the tops of their skulls . . .

V

Far, far below, the situation was no less tense, if somewhat less hectic.

"Captain, I believe that for the first time they are making an effort to transmit a comprehensible thought pattern toward us," Spock told them. "Our speculation as to the relationship between age and size appears to have been correct. They are worried about their child, the one caught in the transporter beam.

"These, I gather, are the parents of the missing one. Despite the lack of external sexual characteristics, the standard male-female partnership is in existence here."

"Never mind the biological details, Mr. Spock," a tense Kirk ordered, eyeing the two silent Lactrans warily. "While they're worried about their offspring, I'm more concerned about what it might do to the *Enterprise*. Even an adolescent probably possesses considerable mental as well as physical powers."

"What in Carrel's scalpel went wrong, though?" a bemused McCoy wondered.

"I'm not sure, Bones. Obviously Scotty received our call for help, a call that was sorely lacking in details. That thing snatched the communicator before I could give him any details. As soon as the alien took the communicator from me, well, it was still activated when it was grabbed away. Scotty centered on it, of course."

Spock was swaying slightly, drifting deeper into trance. "They seem to think you made the child disappear," he murmured, "since you were the one who operated the device. Their reaction . . . their reaction . . ."

"Go on, Spock."

"They are surprised, and concerned. The concern is for their missing offspring. They are surprised because we had not been classed as either an intelligent or a dangerous species. And they are somewhat shocked to discover that we may be both."

"We can't stand here," McCoy said nervously, "we've got to do something . . . or they will."

Kirk tried to calm the jittery McCoy. In fact, everyone appeared increasingly nervous. That could only make the Lactrans worry more about their child.

"Calm down . . . all of you. Let's not give our captors cause for concern. The best thing we can do is—"

He doubled over and fell to the ground, twisting in pain—and this time he wasn't acting.

"Jim!" McCoy was at his side, feeling helpless. "What is it?"

"My head! Inside . . . my head." The words came out with an effort. "I think . . . the baby. What happened to the baby?"

There was an odd, hollow tone in those last words, as if something unhuman was trying to operate a human voice mechanism.

"Fight it, Captain," Spock urged, "fight it as hard as you can. Don't try to listen, don't try to let them use you." He turned to McCoy.

"They think so fast, their patterns of cogitation are so complicated, that their own thoughts are too complex for a human brain to assimilate." He watched as Kirk rolled to his knees, tried to keep his balance, and failed.

"If he gives up, even for a moment," Spock explained with deathly precision, "he may go mad. The Lactran thought processes will overload his neural capacity."

M'ress uttered a sound halfway between a screech and a feline yowl as the Lactran, still holding Scott firmly in its grasp, charged out of the turbolift onto the bridge. Arex rose from his position at the navigation console, but despite the shock and consternation, no one moved to abandon his post, no one ran for an exit.

And that was the last thing Scott wanted, since the presence of others seemed to make his captor nervous. The chief engineer had been treated to one of the slug-thing's mental assaults and had no desire to endure another.

"Everyone clear out," he ordered, seeing that no one was going to budge without being told to do so. "Don't antagonize it."

"Antagonize what?" M'ress asked quietly, bearing Scott's admonition in mind. "What *is* that thing?"

"I don't know . . . yet. But it hasn't injured anyone badly . . . yet. And I have the impression it doesn't want to. It could have sent pieces of me all over the ship by now but hasn't taken that option." The Lactran headed toward the center of the bridge. As it began to move, the bridge personnel started to edge around toward the turbolift doors.

"All rright, what do you want us to do, sirr?" M'ress queried, standing by the open doors.

"Just leave quietly, lassie. Report to Lieutenant Seelens, tell her to set up security teams on all transporters. I don't expect any more visitors, but I want to be ready to greet them in case I'm wrong."

"Yes, sirr," she acknowledged. "But what arre you going to do, sirr?"

Scott let out a resigned sigh. "What do you think, Lieutenant? Whatever it wants me to."

M'ress filed into the lift behind Arex, turned, and started to say something. The closing doors cut her off soundlessly.

He was alone on the bridge with the alien invader.

The front end of the creature waved back and forth, like an elephant sensing the air. It slid forward and placed Scott in the command chair—gently and right-side up, the chief noted with thanks—and then turned its featureless front to stare at him.

"Now look," Scott began, "supposin' you and I talk this over?"

No response from the slug.

"You can talk, can't you?"

Silence, and that continuing eyeless gaze.

"If you can't talk, how do you communicate?" He tried Federation sign language. "Well, what can you do?"

The creature turned and began examining the control consoles nearby, beginning with navigation and working its way around to Spock's library-computer station. The tail end touched several switches, and the multiple screens at the station lit and began pouring forth a torrent of information. Scott couldn't even identify the sections the creature was studying, much less follow its progress.

"Listen, you've got to be careful here," he explained patiently. "This is the control room of a—hey!"

The tail had reached out and lifted him again, then replaced him in the chair. If this was the alien's method of indicating one should be silent, it failed to impress Scott. The chief was growing increasingly nervous as the alien continued to touch this or that control.

"Now, look," he began as the Lactran switched off the library and moved around to face the helm and navigation consoles, "just keep your grubby little whatever-it-is off things you don't under . . . *no, don't touch that!*"

Too late. The multitipped tail was moving across the consoles with blurring speed, far too fast for Scott to follow. It touched switches, pushed buttons and levers, activated telltales, and checked readouts, while its front end slowly weaved back and forth from one console to the other.

"Listen," Scott howled desperately, "if you keep that up, you'll send us runnin' off to the back of wherever!"

His attention was diverted by the already altered picture on the main viewscreen. It was anything but reassuring. It showed a rapidly shrinking green and white globe, Lactra VII, become a pinhead circle instead of a screen-filling orb.

Seconds later the warp-drive was engaged. An enraged, horrified Scott could only stare and hurl Highland imprecations at the gray hippo before him. His horror sprang from the knowledge that any idiot could activate the *Enterprise*'s warp-drive engines; but the matter of navigation, of determining where those engines were taking the ship, was a chore for experience and expertise.

And he had the sick feeling that the voiceless mass in front of him had neither.

The two Lactrans abruptly turned from the enclosure to converse with each other. Simultaneously, Kirk's body relaxed. His face was pale and his tunic drenched with perspiration. As the others watched anxiously, he rolled over, sat up, and let out a long *whoosh* of exhaustion.

"Have they stopped, Jim?" McCoy finally asked, when he felt Kirk had recovered enough to answer. The captain looked like a man who had just come out of an eighteen-hour sleep. "How are you?"

"They've left off . . . for now," Kirk told them. "I think I'm okay, Bones. But I'm tired . . . so tired."

"Understandable," McCoy agreed. "Spock, what do you think of . . . Spock?" McCoy turned, to see Spock staring as if frozen at the pair of concerned Lactrans. He was startled to see three more of the full-sized aliens sidling up to the first two. It seemed the alarm had been raised.

At least, he thought grimly, they had succeeded in getting their captors to notice them.

Spock left his trance and glanced down at Kirk. "I am not certain, Captain, but I believe they have concluded that they cannot break into your mind on an individual or even a dualistic basis. They are surprised."

"Good!" McCoy exclaimed. "Maybe they won't try it again."

Spock turned a somber gaze on him. "On the contrary, Doctor, they are now readying the mental strength of five of their number in a more powerful attempt."

A wild, faintly desperate tone underlined Kirk's reaction. "I can't hold out against that many. It's not possible. I don't know why they stopped the last time. You've no idea, Bones, what it's like." He turned an anxious stare on the gathering of Lactrans.

"I don't know if I'll come out of another attack like that last one, let alone one of more than twice the strength."

"Every one of us must help the captain," Spock instructed. "Concentrate on him, try to become one with him, a part of his mind and thoughts. Perhaps we can create some kind of screen, or at least—"

But Kirk was already on the ground again, spinning in pain and screaming for something to leave him alone.

"It's tearing—!"

Their concern was too great for those surrounding him to erect anything like an effective mental screen, if such a thing were even possible. Kirk rolled about for several minutes until his body quit. He lay still, only a quivering of arms and legs and an occasional jerk of his head indicating that his spread-eagled form was still fighting back.

His continued resistance was as obvious as the fact that he was slowly weakening. More minutes passed. Kirk rolled onto his face, limp as a rag doll now, his form twitching from time to time as if touched by a live cable.

A number of wholly alien feelings were approaching eruption inside the *Enterprise's* first officer when a familiar and unexpected glow appeared in the air inside the force screen, as if someone were shining a colored light on a rippling sheet of clear silk.

Two figures began to emerge. "The Lactrans are coming into the enclosure," Markel began, "but why in this fashion if—"

He broke off as the shifting hues solidified. One of the two figures was Lactran, all right. But the other . . .

It was a surprise to see the small Lactran reappear, but it was a positive shock to see Chief Engineer Scott held firmly in its tail-grip.

The surprise and shock worked equally on the five Lactrans outside the field. Their concentration was shattered by the appearance of the small one, and the results were immediately apparent as Kirk finally ceased his helpless spasms.

The adolescent put Scott down gently. As soon as the chief had moved off a bit, two of the larger Lactrans—not even Spock could tell if they were the original two—reached in and drew the smaller one outside the boundary of the force screen. Rather roughly, McCoy thought, as he turned his attention back to the still supine Kirk.

The others were already gathered around him. He turned onto his back, and McCoy saw his eyes were glazed. Slowly, he tried to sit up, but nearly collapsed. McCoy bent to help.

"No, I'm all right, I'm okay," he muttered thickly. But he did not reject the support of McCoy's shoulder after he had struggled to his feet. His eyes were clearing rapidly.

"Whew! I feel like my brain's been pulled through a wringer." He looked around at the assemblage of worried faces. "You've no idea what it's like, Scotty." He blinked. "Scotty? What are you doing here?"

The chief jerked his head to indicate the activity behind them. "My alien acquaintance brought me."

Spock looked incredulous, though his words were as evenly modulated as ever. "You succeeded in making contact with it?"

"Not exactly." The object of sudden startled attention grinned. "It made contact with me. I gather it was a tremendous effort for the poor child to slow down to my level."

"You were right, Mr. Spock. Our attempts at communication were properly directed, only at the wrong members of this society."

"What did you learn?" Kirk asked.

The chief engineer considered the question carefully.

"Some of it doesn't translate verra easily into human terms," he explained slowly. "But I did succeed in grasping a few definite concepts.

"For one, our small friend is the emotional and physical Lactran equivalent of a human six-year-old. Mentally, however, it is considerably superior to any of us. The first thing it did on appearin' on board was pick the nearest mind for useful information. *Mine!* Then it went on and absorbed all the knowledge in the ship's library computer, science center, and general storage facility. Bein' a curious laddie—or lassie—it decided to play around with its new toys. That included operating the ship's helm. Sent us tearin' right out of orbit."

Kirk, who saw the *Enterprise* gallivanting all over known space at the mercy of a playful alien infant, swallowed hard. "How did you convince it to come back?"

Scott turned introspective. "I think it was my concern for the rest of the crew that persuaded it. That, and the fact that I never showed any hatred toward it." He shrugged. "I suppose any child can tell instinctively when a threat is present and when it's not. And there was my willingness, the willingness of another, uh, child, to chat with it."

"Infant-to-infant communication," Spock observed, showing no resentment at being likewise classified. "My congratulations, Mr. Scott."

"Anyhow," the chief continued, "I managed to convince it that I wasn't anybody's pet, and that we're no mere grubbers in the dirt. And that it would be a sight better for all concerned if it would bring the ship back into orbit around its own home world. From there, it wasn't too hard to convince it to reenter the transporter so we could return home. By that time the youngster was pretty sure I meant it no harm. What finally reassured it was my readiness to come along too. I think they can sense friendliness in another's thoughts as readily as they can much more complicated concepts. If we could only—"

Spock cut him off softly. "A moment, please, Mr.

Scott." The *Enterprise*'s first officer shook his head irritably, like a man trying to throw off the first assault of an advancing migraine. "I believe ... they are trying to contact us directly. I can ... make out ... something. It is very difficult. The adults ... so concise, so fast in their mental formulations ...

"They are ... trying now ... to slow down for us. Communication involves the insertion of many transitional concepts they have long since discarded as superfluous. The ... child ... has explained to them. Adults are attempting to rephrase their normal thoughts into ... babytalk." The evident irritation and minor pain gradually faded, while his attitude of attentive listening remained unchanged.

"There ... it's better now. The child has learned much from us, particularly from Mr. Scott. It has also acquired an enormous volume of information about us, and is relaying this to its parents ... though I can recognize only glimpses and snatches of what it is relating. It is like trying to follow every ripple in a fast-flowing stream." A pause; then: "It has concluded, Captain. Already it has told its parents all about the Federation and the many aspects of its composition, including all the races it comprises."

"Already," gulped McCoy, wondering not merely at a youthful mind capable of delivering a torrent of material so rapidly, but also at those more mature minds able to absorb and assimilate it.

At the moment, however, there were other concerns tempering Kirk's admiration of the Lactrans' mental calisthenics.

"All that information ought to include enough facts about ourselves to convince them we're not common animals. How do they look at us now, Mr. Spock?"

"It would appear that they have indeed revised their initial opinions of us," Spock replied, swaying slightly as he struggled to codify the Lactrans' rapid flow of thoughts. "Apparently we are now classed as simplistic life forms in the process of evolving rapidly into a higher order."

"Vulcans included?" McCoy couldn't resist the opportunity.

Spock's intense concentration didn't keep him from sounding slightly annoyed. "Yes, Vulcans included." He frowned as the Lactrans continued to relay information.

"They are confused now."

"That's a hopeful sign," Kirk murmured. "I was beginning to wonder if they were infallible."

"It would seem not, Captain. Several of them are arguing that on closer inspection we may prove in certain unexpected ways to be equal or even superior to them. I cannot follow all of the discussion, but much of it involves the efficacy of instinct as opposed to pure thought."

"No need to ask which of those we're supposed to represent!" McCoy snorted. "I don't know if they're flattering us or insulting us."

"It is purely a zoological question to them, Doctor," Spock explained. "The question of value judgment does not enter into it."

"I can see why they're using you as their go-between," McCoy murmured, but so softly that no one else could hear. Aloud, he observed, "So they think that as far as we're concerned, equality is just around the corner?"

Spock nodded absently, as usual taking no notice of the doctor's sarcasm.

"At the moment I'm more interested in getting back on the *Enterprise* than in reaching their mental level," Kirk declared pointedly. To McCoy's professional gaze the captain appeared and sounded fully recovered from the withering Lactran mind probe which had almost rendered him comatose.

Kirk had no time to consider the speed of his recovery. It had occurred to him that, despite the Lactrans' apparent reconsideration of their human captives, they might find other reasons for not releasing them.

"How do we manage that return—or do we?"

Another pause followed while Spock listened to intense Lactran babytalk and strove to comprehend. If such delays were merely irritating to Kirk, to Markel and Bryce they seemed interminable.

"It appears that we do," the first officer finally informed them. Bryce began to smile. "Under one condition." The smile died aborning.

"While we are still classified as beneath Lactrans on the scale of evolution, they do concede that we do not belong in their zoo. We grade high in certain abilities and low in others. This appparent contradiction continues to puzzle them."

"That's hardly surprising," observed McCoy. "The contradictions within ourselves have been confusing mankind since the beginning of its history."

"What's this condition they're talking about?" Kirk asked, somehow sensing that it involved more than the Lactran equivalent of a handshake. Their captors had some purpose in mind.

He would never have guessed it in a hundred years.

But the Lactrans refused to be hurried.

"Their abstract imagery . . . so difficult to interpret." Again a frown of intense concentration contorted the first officer's face. "They do not feel that those who maintain zoos belong in them."

"I wouldn't have put it that way," Markel commented, fairly shaking with impatience. "How do we get out of theirs, then?"

Spock blinked, turned to the Lactrans, and said, "Like this." He walked toward the display table, past where the invisible wall had been, and over to the table itself. There was no hum, whine, or revealing flash to announce the abrupt termination of the restraining force field. One moment it was present, and the next it simply was not.

Still pondering the mysterious condition under which the Lactrans would agree to release them, Kirk followed his first officer's lead. McCoy, Scott, and Markel followed him. Lieutenant Bryce hesitated, then turned and started back toward the house to rouse the still weak Randolph.

As the former captives left the enclosure, the front ends of all five Lactrans turned in unison to follow them with almost mechanical precision—attentively,

Kirk thought. While he could not be sure, he was willing to bet that their captors were prepared to prevent any sudden "instinctive" surprises—such as a rapid attempt to beam back up to the ship.

Eyeless stares followed the movements of the humans as they picked up activated phasers, tricorders, and other equipment. Kirk did not miss the expression on Markel's face as the leader of the survey team lovingly fondled the familiar instruments he had longed for these past weeks. There was much more to the way he checked out the devices, replacing many on his belt and survey suit, than simple pleasure at regaining denied possessions. They no longer had the significance given them by captivity, but regaining them held a symbolic significance far greater. Markel found a freedom in handling Federation devices manufactured by Federation machinery and hands, instead of falsely familiar constructs manufactured by an alien keeper.

The survey commander had ample time to indulge himself in the inspection of his lost equipment, because it took some time for Lieutenant Randolph, aided by Bryce, to join them. When she finally appeared, McCoy hurried forward to examine her, moving his hands toward his medikit. She shook off the incipient attention.

"Please, Doctor, no drugs. I want to savor every second of our departure from this place. I promise not to collapse until it's into a Federation bed." McCoy hesitated, then smiled and nodded understandingly.

Kirk tried to appear interested in the remaining survey instruments, but his attention was actually focused on the Lactrans, who appeared to be observing the byplay between McCoy and Randolph. The captain's hand shifted imperceptibly toward the communicator, which once more rested in its familiar place at his side.

The movement was not as imperceptible as he thought, however, because as his fingers touched the smooth edge of the device, the front end of one of the watching adults turned toward him. The fingers slid on past and above the communicator to scratch easily at his belly. He sighed reluctantly. So much for trying to beam clear from under the mental gaze of *these* jailers.

"Very well, Mr. Spock, let's have the details of this condition. I give my word we'll abide by whatever they have in mind." Easy enough to do, he mused sardonically, without a hope of otherwise departing. For a brief moment, he thought he sensed an alien mental laugh.

Spock strained again, beginning to show some signs of fatigue. The process of acting as translator was starting to wear on him.

"It is still difficult, Captain. Their thought processes are so incredibly fast. It is becoming slightly easier, though. We are learning from each other as we continue to communicate. Somehow, I gain the impression that the condition in some way involves this 'zoo'—not quite the proper term, but it must serve."

"If they think we're going to volunteer some substitute exhibits," McCoy began heatedly.

"No, no, Doctor . . . it does not involve the continued presence of humans, Vulcans, or any other Federation-member race."

McCoy calmed down, satisfied.

"It is more complex than that."

"How so, Mr. Spock?" Kirk pressed curiously. The first officer had turned to face the largest of the adult Lactrans.

"I am told by the Old One that their collection is not complete. It will probably never be complete, since the desire for expansion and acquisition has faded on Lactra. There are temporal referents that I do not understand. The Old One explains gently that this does not matter. Apparently, one especially desired creature is overdue for collection. It is this that they wish us to help rectify."

"One creature?" McCoy echoed uncertainly. "You mean, they want our help in capturing some unknown specimen?"

"Essentially, that is correct, Doctor. It seems that there is one creature they have known about for hundreds of our years yet have not been able to capture because"—the young Lactran moved jerkily, and Spock turned to gaze blankly in its direction—"because they have given up the knowledge of how to construct artificial devices—ships like the *Enterprise*—capable of ranging deep space. They have been content in past centuries to range for specimens close to their own system, and to use the years for refining their mind control. The emphasis in Lactran society has shifted during this period from the practical to the purely aesthetic.

"Yet they still retain knowledge of this one special creature, and wish to obtain a live example of it. It is for this that they request our aid."

Kirk considered gratefully the courtesy of the Lactrans. That they could as easily take control of the *Enterprise* as request the voluntary help of its crew was something he did not doubt. But for some reason it was important to them that such help be given freely.

McCoy walked close. He whispered cautioningly, "I wouldn't be too ready to accept their claim that they've 'forgotten' how to build deep-space ships, Jim."

"If it's an evasion, Bones, there's not much we can do about it. We can either believe them or call them liars. I don't think it would be wise to do the latter. They obviously have their reasons for wanting the use of the *Enterprise* . . . and us."

"Then consider this," the doctor persisted. "If the Lactrans, with all their amply demonstrated abilities, their mental powers, and considerable technology, have been unable to capture this boojum so far, what makes them think we can do any better?"

"Good point, Bones," Kirk agreed willingly. "Transportation we can provide, and we have had some experience handling live alien specimens—everything from tribbles to wauls. But interstellar big-game hunters we're not." He looked back at his first officer, and his voice rose.

"Explain to them, Spock, that we agree. We're willing to aid in any way we can, in return for our eventual safe departure from Lactra. How should we begin? Do they have any idea where to start looking for this prize creature? We certainly have no experience of it, or the Lactran youngster would have discovered some reference to it during its *very* thorough examination of our library."

"On the contrary, Captain," explained a listening Spock, "they say we have looked upon the jawanda without seeing it—'jawanda' is the nearest pronunciation-conceptualization they can provide. The actual name is quite unpronounceable.

"Locating one of the creatures is not the difficulty. It is the method of capture, which requires apparatus of a very special type which the Lactrans do not have access to. Nor do we, I am told. Such apparatus is beyond our technology."

"Then how in blazes do they expect us to bring one of these indescribable whatsises back?" McCoy wanted to know.

Spock explained slowly. "To do this we must travel with them to a world known as Boqu. When the Lactrans traveled the Long Crawling past far-distant worlds many *ghids* ago, they chanced on this planet of the Boqus. These people had developed a method of controlling the jawanda. It is the Lactrans' hope that they have not lost that knowledge."

"Hope?" asked Kirk. "Don't they know for sure?"

"No, Captain. There has been no contact between Lactra and Boqu for several *minaghids*."

"*Mina*—how long is that?" McCoy queried, trying to make some sense out of all this talk of jawandas and *ghids* and such.

"It is not precisely—"

"Translatable," the doctor finished for him. "I know, I know."

"But it is a considerable time," Spock concluded.

Kirk thought rapidly, gazing idly at the display table. If the Boqus had lost the required knowledge, the *Enterprise* would simply return its passengers to Lactra. Boqu might not even be inhabited any longer. Or, despite the Lactrans' encyclopedic store of information, their story could turn out to be a myth accepted as truth.

Nonetheless, it would be even better if he could talk the Lactrans out of the idea. He was very much aware of the compound behind them, its falsely attractive little houses and grounds waiting ominously to rewelcome the recent tenants. The Lactrans could force them back into that landscaped cage as easily as let them leave. He would have to be careful.

"Explain that we would do our utmost to help, Mr. Spock, but that the *Enterprise* has no facilities for the housing and the care of unknown zoological specimens. Even if we managed to capture one of these jawanda creatures, it could die for lack of proper care on the way back to Lactra."

Another of those nerve-tingling silences ensued while he awaited Spock's version of the alien's reply. It was unexpected.

"Their initial reaction—I cannot be positive, of course, Captain, but it seems to be one of mirth. Now the explanation-reply is coming through. They assure us that it will not even be necessary to utilize the *Enterprise* to transport the jawanda. The capture method itself, by its very nature as well as the nature of the jawanda, handles all problems of transportation and care."

Well, it had been worth a try, Kirk reflected. "It all sounds reasonable," he replied guardedly. "How do we go about finding this mysterious Boqu? I've never heard mention of such a world. And, assuming we *can* locate it, how do we contact the local population and go about explaining what we need?"

"They are not surprised at our ignorance," Spock countered. "Boqu is not an easy world to locate, nor one we would stumble upon in the course of normal exploration. As to finding the planet, as well as to the problems of contacting the Boqus and making the request, they have a simple solution.

"Two of them are going to come with us."

VI

This time it was Kirk's eyebrows which rose in surprise. "I see," he muttered. The thought of having a couple of Lactran superminds on board the *Enterprise*, minds which could at any time take control of the ship, was not a comforting one.

Not that he had any choice, if he did not want to experience the cold comforts of the force cage again. He battled with himself, uncomfortably aware that his answer was awaited.

What was he so worried about, after all? Now that the aliens had been apprised of the actual intelligence of their former captives, now that they were actively seeking their cooperation, what reason to suspect treachery? He could not think of one. Naturally, that set him immediately to try to conjure half a dozen threatening possibilities.

While the captain was debating himself, Spock cocked his head slightly to one side, like a man striving to make sure of something just overheard.

"It appears," the first officer announced finally, "that we may be host to three rather than two Lactrans. The pair which have been selected to come with us are the parents of the young Lactran who was accidentally beamed aboard ship. The youngster is presently arguing vociferously with his parents, insisting that he be allowed to accompany the expedition."

"Doesn't make much difference, I suppose," murmured McCoy. "Two Lactrans or three."

"Our feelings have nothing to do with it, Doctor," Spock informed him. "It is the elder Lactrans' concern which opposes the youth's desire to participate." A pause; then: "They are trying to explain to their offspring that this undertaking is potentially too dangerous to permit it to come along."

McCoy stopped his nervous pacing and glanced up sharply. "Hey, if this is too dangerous for a Lactran youngster, who's already shown he's capable of taking over the ship, I'm not sure I want to—"

Kirk cut him off. "We have little choice, Bones—remember?" His attention was drawn to Scott. Strangely, the chief engineer was grinning. "You find the situation amusing, Scotty?"

"What? Well, part of it, Captain, yes. I canna follow the chatter of the adults, like Mr. Spock, but I have a bit of a rapport with the youngster. He overheard what Dr. McCoy just said. Now he's tellin' his parents that if they don't allow him to come along, then *we* might consider the trip too dangerous for *us*. So they have to take him along to convince us."

Kirk found himself smiling in response. "Not only precocious, but a budding diplomat. How is his argument going over, Mr. Spock?"

The first officer replied slowly. "Very well, it would seem, Captain. The adults acknowledge the validity of the youth's claims, which is more important to them than our possible refusal. They could force us to do their bidding"—Kirk shuddered in remembrance of the mental assault he'd so recently endured—"but feel that for two already stated reasons this would not be right: because we are not animals, and because the success of the undertaking requires full and enthusiastic cooperation on both sides."

"We've already consented to cooperate, Mr. Spock," Kirk replied readily, "though I can't vouch for our enthusiasm. All right, we'll aid them in capturing a single jawanda, whatever it is, and in returning it and them to Lactra. That will discharge our obligation to them." He did not bother to ask what assurance the Lactrans would give that they would adhere to their end of the bargain. He could not very well force them into anything. The men of the Federation were entering into a possibly dangerous situation on faith, a course acceptable only because of the absence of alternatives.

But he was curious. "What kind of guarantee do they want to insure that we'll follow through on our part of the agreement?"

Spock frowned as though Kirk had said something betraying ignorance of the obvious. "They see the honesty of your response in your mind, Captain. No further assurance is necessary. They are appalled that such a thing could be considered."

Kirk grunted; he was satisfied. "So much for intangibles. Getting down to basics"—he studied the huge bulk of the adult Lactrans—"we come to the matter of accommodations."

"They say you have no reason to worry, Captain," the first officer declared. "While their society may appear complex, it is actually as simple as their needs. From what their offspring has told them of the *Enterprise*, they feel they will be quite comfortable in an empty cargo hold. They see no reason why our food synthesizers cannot produce nourishment acceptable to their systems. Other than this, they anticipate nothing in the way of special requirements even if the trip should prove one of extended duration."

"That's a relief," Kirk answered feelingly, leaving aside for the moment the troubling question of what constituted a journey of "extended duration" for a Lactran.

Just how far away *was* this Boqu?

McCoy had sidled over close to him. "Just had a worrisome thought, Jim."

"Only one?" Kirk managed the first real smile in days. "What is it now?"

"We're supposed to be carrying out a straightforward rescue mission. Before too much more time passes, Starfleet Headquarters is liable to get nervous about the absence of reports. What do we tell them if they manage to contact us?" He nodded once, significantly, toward the silent Lactrans.

Kirk shrugged. "They'll assume we're still searching for Lieutenant Commander Markel and his ship. If anyone inquires beyond that . . ." He paused thoughtfully. "We needn't go into details. Sometimes a starship captain has to make treaties with newly met races without the aid of formal diplomacy, has to create procedure in order to respond to exigencies not covered in the manuals. Our agreement to cooperate with the Lactrans has the status of a temporary treaty."

"Under what classification?" McCoy inquired relentlessly.

"Expediency." The captain's smile vanished as Kirk considered exactly what they might be getting themselves into. "Maybe it would be better to tell the truth and, if anyone asks, say we've gone a-hunting. I wish we knew for what."

"The Lactrans are prepared, Captain," Spock informed him. "They have given in to their young, and it will accompany them. If all is in readiness, they are anxious to depart."

Kirk wasn't anxious, but saw no excuse for further delay. He spoke to Scott. "Tell Chief Kyle to beam us back aboard, making allowance for three regular-size guests and three large ones." He gestured toward the Lactrans.

The chief engineer already had his communicator out and open. "All right, Captain."

"And have the chief use the transporter nearest Shuttle Bay for our Lactran visitors. The corridors are larger there and will make it easier for them to move around, if they so desire."

Scott nodded assent and relayed the instructions to the ship. The Lactrans appeared thoroughly absorbed as several of the humans vanished. Then they themselves were gone, accompanied by Kirk and Spock.

Once back on board the *Enterprise,* Kirk's first concern was to make certain the Lactrans were comfortably ensconced in their temporary quarters. Despite the sterility of the surroundings in the empty cargo hold, they professed to be quite satisfied with the amenities.

Leaving Spock to tend to any immediate alien requests, Kirk made his way quickly to Sick Bay. McCoy and Nurse Chapel were already well along in their detailed examination of the three surviving explorers.

"Markel and Bryce are in excellent shape, Jim," the doctor told him, "as would befit valuable exhibits."

"And Lieutenant Randolph?"

"She'll be all right eventually, but she needs about a month of doing nothing." McCoy grinned. "Sometimes that's the hardest prescription to assign. She's an active type, physically and mentally, and it's going to be difficult to keep her confined in a bed." The smile faded, to be replaced by a look of concern. "Confined she'll be, though. Her system is badly weakened."

"It may be improved when the official report reaches Starfleet, Bones. Endurance under conditions of stress is often grounds for promotion. At least you won't have to worry about the jawanda—assuming we can find and capture such a creature. The Lactrans are convinced it won't require any kind of attention. Spock is still trying to draw the details of the animal out of them, but the conceptualizations, as he keeps putting it, are confusing. Also, some of our preconceptions about jawandas appear to amuse our guests no end."

"I'm glad they think it's funny," McCoy observed wryly, indicating that he saw very little humor in the situation. His gaze, revealingly, was on the bedridden Randolph. "I haven't exactly warmed up to our elephantine guests."

"Think friendly thoughts, Bones," Kirk advised him strongly, reminding him of the Lactrans' mental abilities.

Satisfied that the three survivors were okay, Kirk headed for the bridge. Jawanda, jawanda . . . the name meant nothing to him. He could not even vaguely relate it to any creature he had ever heard of. Well, the Lactrans would have to clarify the nature of their quarry soon enough. There was no real need to worry so long as it wasn't going to be transported on board the ship.

It didn't occur to Kirk to consider the possibility that perhaps, for certain reasons, it could not be.

Spock and McCoy were waiting for him when he returned to the bridge. Their presence was expected; that of their new companion was not.

"I was about to order the installation of a special intercom unit for the use of the adult Lactrans in the converted hold, Captain," explained the first officer, "so that they would be in constant communication with us. They informed me that this was not only unnecessary, but a waste of equipment." He gestured at the long gray mass near the science station, the front end of which was presently exploring Spock's instrumentation.

"Their offspring will remain on the bridge. As it is always in telepathic contact with its parents, it can convey their impressions to us and a description of what takes place on the bridge to them instantaneously, without the need for, as they put it, awkward mechanical contrivances. He fits into the turbolifts, while the adults do not."

"Thank the adults for their consideration, Mr. Spock," Kirk told him. While he was not thrilled by the prospect of having a superintelligent child underfoot for the duration of the journey, he could not deny the logic behind its presence.

While it might be unnecessary, there was something else he ought to do. Moving to the command chair, Kirk activated the interdeck communications network and addressed the pickup:

"Attention, all personnel. This is the captain speaking. We are about to embark on an expedition of indeterminate length to perform a service for our newfound friends, the Lactrans, inhabitants of the planet about which we are orbiting. Concurrent with this, we will have as our guests three representatives of that race. Several of you have already noticed their arrival on board. The Lactrans are natural telepaths and . . . curious. The actions of an alien life form, or its shape, should not prove offensive to any of you or you wouldn't be part of this crew.

"Two adult Lactrans are presently installed in temporary quarters in cargo hold Fourteen-B. A third, an adolescent of the species, is at present with me on the bridge, but it has been given the run of the ship." He forbore adding that there was no way he could restrict the youthful alien's activities. It was only good diplomacy to grant gracious assent to the inevitable.

"Bear in mind that this is the young, however intelligent, of a species. It may be inclined to act in sometimes inexplicable fashion. Rest assured that, however misdirected, such actions are in no way hostile. I stress this so that no one will react in a manner in any way other than friendly toward our guests." So that, he finished silently, our guests don't get peeved and decide to take over the ship.

Ending the transmission, he rose again and spoke to the helm: "Stand by to get underway, Mr. Sulu."

"Standing by, sir," the helmsman acknowledged.

"Spock, Bones—let's go greet our passengers and find out the details of this expedition."

The two adult Lactrans were lolling about the cargo hold, apparently somnolent. Spock assured Kirk and McCoy that, despite the appearance of inactivity, the minds of both adults were as active and alert as ever. As he sat down, Kirk felt a tingling probe at the back of his skull and knew the correctness of the first officer's announcement.

He had expected the young Lactran to accompany them for this formal explanatory session, but the youngster had chosen to remain on the bridge, in the company of Engineer Scott. Several members of the crew had already remarked that the young alien followed Scott around like a dog attending its master.

"Before you enjoy that analogy," the chief engineer had responded, "keep in mind that in this case the 'dog' is twenty times smarter than the 'master.'"

Glancing approvingly around the hold, Kirk saw that Scotty's technicians had installed some recreational simulacrum machinery. Despite their insistence that nothing in the way of material comfort was required, he thought he sensed the Lactrans' approval at the way in which the "simplistic" machinery projected three-dimensional reproductions of the Lactran surface on the bare metal walls.

"They are indeed pleased, Captain," Spock informed him, unnervingly confirming his unspoken supposition, "though more by our concern for their comfort than by the actual projections themselves."

Kirk shifted in his chair. "If everyone's comfortable, then perhaps they can give us a course?"

"Naturally, Captain." Spock paused a moment, then replied, sooner than Kirk had expected, "They apparently have already done so."

There was a buzz from the cargo-hold intercom, and Kirk rose to answer it. "Kirk here."

"Captain"—it was Sulu's voice: excited, confused, and just a bit awed—"someting just jumped inside my head. It was—"

"A series of coordinates," Kirk finished for him, turning to study the impassive Lactrans respectfully.

"Yes, sir—but how did you know?"

"Never mind that, Mr. Sulu. Were the coordinates precise?"

"Very, Captain."

"That's our new course, then. Lay them in. All ahead warp-factor four."

"Yes sir," the helmsman replied, his tone slightly dazed. "Bridge out."

Kirk walked back to the chair and resumed his seat slowly. "Mr. Spock?"

"The adults relayed the information to their offspring, Captain, the moment they sensed the request in your mind. The youth, in turn, planted them clearly in the thoughts of Lieutenant Sulu."

"Wonderful communications system," observed McCoy, a mite sourly, feeling even more left out of things than usual.

"I presume the terminus of those coordinates is Boqu?" Kirk commented, expecting a casual assent. It wasn't quite forthcoming.

"The Lactrans hope so, Captain," Spock told him. It took barely a second for the import of that reply to sink in.

"Hope?" a startled Kirk blurted quickly. "What do they mean, 'hope'? I understood that they knew exactly where this world lies!"

Spock was shaking his head slowly, his eyes half glazed. "They do and yet they do not, Captain. It was such a long time ago that the last Lactran ship went out to Boqu. The records involved are quite old. The coordinates should lead us directly to Boqu, but the Lactrans cannot say this for certain. For various reasons its position in the plenum is not easy to plot."

"What," Kirk went on, taking a long, slow breath, "if Boqu doesn't exist where these ancient coordinates insist it's supposed to?"

This time Spock's reply was longer in coming. "If that is the case, the Lactrans say, we will have to begin a search for its present location."

Kirk started to object, then caught himself. It was impossible to tell what the aliens might consider an unfriendly gesture. Pointing out to them that the *Enterprise* could not spend an infinite number of years looking for a world that might be only an old rumor might so be interpreted. Which led him uncomfortably back to the possibility of the *Enterprise*'s operating under Lactran control, without his cooperation.

He saw the *Enterprise* spiraling farther and farther out from an empty point in space, stopping only to take on fresh supplies at support bases, to pick up new dilithium crystals and power elements. He watched their Lactran hosts insist on a continuation of the search, the ship's crew growing older and older in pursuit of a mythical planet ... How long did Lactrans live, anyway? He suspected that it was well beyond the normal human or even Vulcan life span.

It would be best to shunt that unpleasant scenario aside and hope that the Lactrans' ancient records were as remarkable as their mental powers.

"Now that we know where we're going," he declared to Spock, and thus to the pair of watching aliens, "perhaps we can have some more information on what exactly it is we're going for? Can they describe one of these jawandas for us?"

Spock, attentive, recited slowly, as though from the pages of an old, old book: "A jawanda is a large, asexual creature of unusual appearance with interesting coloring." He blinked and looked across at the other two officers. "That's all."

McCoy grimaced. "That's not very informative, Spock. Couldn't they be a little more descriptive?"

"The Lactrans wish they could, Doctor," the first officer explained. "They indicate that much information is contained in records long since become dust. It is yet another reason why they have been so anxious to secure a specimen for their collection."

Kirk's fingers drummed softly on one arm of the chair. "You said it was a large creature, Mr. Spock. Do the Lactrans know how large?"

Spock assumed an expression of indifference. "It varies considerably from specimen to specimen, it seems. Again, the old records are distressingly poor in detail."

"If information is so scanty," an impatient McCoy muttered, "how do they expect to identify a jawanda? They're not even sure what it looks like." The Lactrans appeared for the first time to confer between themselves.

"They say this does not matter, Doctor," announced Spock languidly, with only a slight frown.

McCoy threw up his hands in a gesture of frustration. "Now how can anyone go hunting for something when they aren't sure of its appearance? Of all the—"

"The Lactrans go on to say, Doctor, that there is even a chance the jawanda looks like nothing."

"I've had it, Jim! Sounds to me like we're on a wild-goose chase—and we're not even sure what the wild goose looks like."

Kirk rose from his chair. "It looks like there's only one way we're going to find out, Bones, and that's to go to Boqu. The answer to the Lactrans' riddle is supposed to lie there. We'll find out the same time they do . . . if we get to the world all right."

"If there *is* a Boqu," grumbled McCoy, rising to join him in leaving the hold.

Silent, the adult Lactrans watched them go.

The following day Kirk entered the bridge determined to locate the world in question. It could be incredibly obscure, but there was still a good chance it circled a sun listed in the star catalog, even if it was it-self as yet unsurveyed.

Already he knew it lay a respectable distance from the Federation periphery. A simple comparison of the coordinates with the many maps locked in his memory had told him that no explored systems were situated in their present path. Even so, the actual figures provided a greater surprise than he'd anticipated. Sitting in the command chair, he studied the printout on the main viewscreen.

"Deeper, Mr. Sulu," he said, and the helmsman re-placed the chart with the star configuration lying be-hind it, and then replaced it again. And again. And yet again. Their present course showed as a glowing red line from one end of each three-dimensional chart to the next without intersecting a single system, without passing near even a postulated solar body.

Finally Kirk was prompted to ask, "Mr. Sulu, are you certain of those coordinates?"

The helmsman looked back over his shoulder and nodded readily. "Absolutely, sir. They appeared in my mind like fluorescent block letters, and remained there until I had them memorized in spite of myself." He shook his head admiringly. "Our visitors convey their information in a manner I envy."

"I see." Kirk studied the uninformative chart projec-tion a moment longer. "Double-check it anyway, please." He turned toward tne science station. "Mr. Spock?"

The first o"icer went into a momentary trance, re-garding the gray mass nearby. Seconds later, Sulu also appeared to drift into a brief dreamlike state before looking back to Kirk.

"No question, sir . . . we're on the course they've in-dicated."

"Thank you, Mr. Sulu. That's all."

Leaning back, the captain considered their present path. A divergence of even a fraction of a degree in one of several directions would have led them to at least three systems, all unexplored but logged. Their actual course, however, was taking them out of the galaxy at approximately a right angle to the galactic ecliptic. No wonder the charts were rapidly growing devoid of stellar phenomena.

"Deeper, Mr. Sulu," he ordered again. The chart was replaced by another, almost blank, save for a few isolated, lonely suns and several drifting nebulae. Beyond was nothing. Absolutely nothing.

"Mr. Spock," he began, looking toward the science station and studiously ignoring the Lactran offspring, "have the Lactrans recheck their memories. Maybe there are several possible locations given in their old records for this planet."

Spock listened to something no one else could hear. Eventually he replied, "They have been monitoring your conversation through their offspring, Captain. They assure me that the coordinates transferred to Mr. Sulu are the only ones given by the ancients for the world known as Boqu."

"Are they aware," Kirk continued gently, "that if we continue on our present course, the first sun we encounter will be an unknown star in M33, the Triangulum Spiral, roughly two point three five *million* light-years away?" He added drily, "If this is the location of Boqu, we won't get there for quite a while."

"While regarding this as a doubtful possibility, Captain, they refuse to discount it," Spock replied. "They are considering it with some interest."

"Not as much as I am," Kirk responded rapidly. "Long before we could reach that system, everyone and everything on board, including the warp-drive engines, would be long dead—the Lactrans included."

"They are aware of this, Captain," Spock continued, listening hard. "They theorize that Boqu must lie somewhat nearer."

"Somewhat?" McCoy muttered nervously.

"There is something else, Captain," the first officer added. "They are wondering if the Boqus will still retain the knowledge and means necessary for capturing a jawanda. They also recall information indicating that the Boqus are a traditionally private folk, and wonder

if they might not also have forgotten their former association with the Lactrans. If this is so, there is always
the possibility of a hostile greeting."

"Charming," Kirk noted dully. "Any other small details like that last one that they might have neglected to
tell us?"

"No, Captain," Spock insisted evenly. "Not at the
moment."

Days lengthened into weeks, with no sign of a possible destination. The *Enterprise* was still running at
warp-four, two factors below her maximum safe cruising speed. Instead of nearing some unexpected system
on the fringe of the galaxy, they drew farther away
from all signs of activity and motion. The last star
marking the boundary of the home galaxy lay far astern.
Kirk had watched it fade from the rear scanners,
a dying beacon, and could not shrug off a sense of
awesome isolation.

More days passed, and Kirk found himself brooding
in the command chair for long hours, staring at the
viewscreen. Long-range scanners focused rearward
showed a falsely dense-seeming arc of brightness behind them: the spiral arm of the galaxy they were
crawling away from. Somewhere back there lay the
Federation, and life in all its swarming multitudes.

Ahead lay a darkness so vast and empty that he felt
like a child tiptoeing into a colossal cavern—the incomprehensible abyss of intergalactic space.

And still the Lactrans insisted stonily that they were
on course for Boqu. Kirk's sense of desperation
reached the point at which he was considering forcing
a confrontation with the starship's imperturbable passengers, even risking a takeover, when a cry came from
the helm:

"Captain, I've got something on the fore sensors!"

"Position, Mr. Sulu?" Kirk inquired, trying to keep
the excitement from his voice.

"Dead on course, sir." A pause; then the uncertain
information, "It appears to be a star, sir, but not much
of a star."

"Confirmed, Captain." Kirk's attention moved to the science station and to Spock, who was staring intently into his gooseneck viewer. "It is a star, with from six to eight companion planets and two belts of asteroidal debris. A KO dwarf, I think, and probably fairly old. Surface temperature low, even for a weak star of its type."

"Anything out here can be classed as a freak, Mr. Spock," Kirk commented interestedly. "Planets it may have, but I don't see how a habitable world could circle a sun that weak. It would have to lie awfully close in, and there would have to be a host of factors compensating for—" he broke off at a loud *humphing* sound from near the science station.

The young Lactran was giving every indication of heightened interest as its front end regarded the screen, which now showed a distant point of white-orange light. Obviously, it was communicating with its parents and with Spock.

"According to all indications," the first officer announced, "that is the Boquian system."

Kirk wanted to believe, but "I don't understand, Mr. Spock. A habitable world out here, circling a sun like this one, and completely isolated from the rest of the galaxy! It staggers the imagination. It's impossible." There was a buzz, and Spock paused long enough to acknowledge a report from belowdecks.

"Not according to the astronomy section, Captain. They cannot wait until we enter the system and they can begin close-in observation."

"You said there were six to eight planets, Mr. Spock," Kirk went on, wishing he could be as unrestrainedly happy as the astronomers. "Which one is Boqu?"

"The old records are barely adequate for identification, Captain. However, I am assured that we will know it when the adults, through the mind of their offspring, sight it."

"Very well. Mr. Sulu, begin survey with the outermost world and take us in one planet at a time."

"Aye, Captain," the helmsman acknowledged.

They moved into the system, passing and rejecting several large dead worlds. Planets five through three proved to be gas giants. The second out from the chill star looked no more promising.

"Boqu," Spock declared firmly, staring fascinatedly at the viewscreen.

"Are you sure, Spock?"

"The Lactrans are, Captain."

Kirk shrugged. "Place us in parking orbit, Mr. Sulu."

"Yes, Captain."

Boqu looked like yet another gas giant, but as they moved nearer the *Enterprise's* sensors began to produce some surprising information.

Boqu possessed certain similarities to Uranus and Jupiter, but it was not a Jovian-type planet. It did put out more radiation than it received from its cinder of a sun. A certain amount of this radiation was being trapped beneath a dense orange cloud layer, heavy with carbon dioxide.

The resultant greenhouse effect was as natural as it was unexpected, creating a surface warm enough to shelter life, though life that would have to be radically different from that on Earth or Vulcan. There was little water vapor and no evidence of free water on the surface.

Boqu was an enormous world, as large as Neptune, but a true planet and not simply a small inner core covered by a huge atmosphere. Yet its gravity was barely half again as Earth's, indicating an absence of heavy metals and a light core.

Still, it was not what Kirk would call a hospitable world. Life-support belts would provide them with warmth, a breathable atmosphere, and protection from strong radiation, but could do nothing to counter the stronger gravity. They would have to handle the strain of one and a half g's as best they were able.

He thought of the Lactrans. Undoubtedly they could tolerate the gravity, but they had evolved on a world similar to Earth. To travel comfortably on the surface of Boqu they would need life-support belts too. Constructing life-support belts for the Lactrans would fall to Mr. Scott's ever inventive staff, but the problem might prove troublesome even to those resourceful minds. Not all the Lactrans' mental prowess would prevail against a poisonous atmosphere. Therefore, the first explorations of Boqu's surface would fall to members of the *Enterprise's* crew—if there was any reason to explore that surface.

Several days of shifting orbit around the planet served only to justify Kirk's initial pessimism. With every scientific instrument on board trained on the surface, they were unable to discover any sign of life.

Kirk became convinced that if anything had ever inhabited this peculiar world, it had long since become extinct. Spock and the Lactrans were not so readily persuaded.

"There could be any number of reasons for our failure to detect life below, Captain," the first officer argued, following another day of fruitless searching. "For one thing, the enormous quantity and variety of radiation the planet is generating makes it extremely difficult for our sensors to separate signs of intelligent surface communication from natural emissions."

"If there *is* any intelligence down there," sniped McCoy.

Spock continued, ignoring the doctor. "Surface conditions on such a world might have forced the inhabitants into other methods of long-range communication."

"It's not only that," a troubled Kirk admitted. "We have instruments capable of piercing the cloud layer. They detect nothing we recognize as motile life on the surface."

"What *we* recognize as life forms a very narrow band in the spectrum of possibilities, Captain."

"A valid point, Spock, but that still leaves us with the problem of identifying *any* life form below." He gestured at the screen, where dense orange-and-pink clouds completely covered a surface many, many times greater in area than Earth's.

"Presumably we could detect life firsthand, but this world is gigantic. To drop below the atmosphere and explore visually from shuttles would take forever." He brooded silently a moment. "What about the Lactrans? Do they have any suggestions?"

"No, Captain," confessed the first officer. "They can add nothing . . . except to reaffirm that this system and this world fit all the ancient descriptions of Boqu. Though they are willing to grant, when I press them, the slim possibility that, for all their reputed knowledge and advanced technology, the Boqus may have become extinct."

"Advanced technology on a world devoid of heavy metals—that's something else I find difficult to swallow," Kirk murmured. "I admit the existence of this world because I'm looking at it, but that's all." His gaze turned to the quiet young Lactran. "Tell the youth to convey this to his parents: We'll circle and study for another of our weeks. If by that time we've turned up *no* evidence of intelligent life, they'll consent to return home." His eyes moved to the rim of the planet, to the total blackness of intergalactic space beyond. No friendly stars formed a perceivable backdrop for this world.

"It's cold out here."

A longer-than-usual wait ensued before the Lactrans replied. Clearly, the guests of the *Enterprise* were struggling through some hard debating among themselves.

"They are reluctant to return empty—a conceptualization I cannot translate, Captain—without a specimen. Yet they do not dispute the validity of your statements. They are agreed. We shall search the surface another week and then we may depart."

"With our obligation to them discharged? We'll leave Lactra's orbit unmolested?"

Spock nodded. "There will be nothing more to restrain us."

The light struck them on the fifth day.

VII

Alarms howled and sensors on the bridge and in all the attentive science stations went berserk as the brilliant beam illumined the *Enterprise* from below, pinioning it in a shaft of intense white radiance powerful enough to pierce the thick clouds. It hit without warning, harmlessly.

When it became apparent that the beam was not dangerous, the brief moment of fear and panic was instantly replaced by curiosity. The radiance was not a gesture of belligerence, but rather the cutting cry of someone shouting, "I'm here, I'm here! Look below, and find me!"

The light vanished, then winked on again. This time instruments other than alarms were ready. The light blinked on and off in regular, obviously unnatural sequence. There was no doubt that it originated from an artificial source.

A source, Kirk mused, of tremendous power, to be able to penetrate that smothering atmosphere and still light up the exterior of the *Enterprise*. The on/off pattern continued for several minutes before halting—permanently, it developed.

"A signal, certainly," Kirk observed, voicing everyone's conclusion aloud. "But why did they break off? Why not continue to guide us down?"

"Perhaps they are incapable of maintaining that strength for very long, Captain" was Spock's comment. "Merely to pierce the cloud layer with such force once is a remarkable feat. To repeat it several times is almost beyond comprehension. Clearly there is intelligence of singular ability still active on the surface below."

Kirk looked to the helm. "Mr. Sulu, did you obtain a fix on the source of the beam?"

The helmsman studied his instrumentation a moment longer before replying. "Yes, Captain—as clear as I was able without actually having direct line of sight to the surface. I'm assuming it traveled outward in a straight line, though it could have been bent or otherwise distorted by some layer in the atmosphere."

"I think not, Lieutenant," countered Spock. "Any beam of sufficient intensity to penetrate that cloud layer and still retain its power of illumination at this distance, apparently undiminished, would likely not be affected by any cloud formation nearer its source."

"We have a destination, then," Kirk noted, rising from the command chair. "Mr. Spock, Dr. McCoy, you'll accompany me to the surface." He nodded at the young Lactran. "Together with our youthful friend, if his parents are agreeable."

Spock's eyebrows arose, and even the Lactran adolescent looked surprised. Kirk felt unaccountably pleased at having been able to startle the seemingly unshakable aliens.

"But how, Jim?" McCoy asked. "Scott's technicians are still working on the problem of life-support belts for Lactrans and—"

"We'll descend in the shuttlecrawler, Bones. It's spacious enough to hold four of us and our young guest, if not either of his much larger parents."

"They are concerned, Captain, but see no reason to object. It is important that they be represented in some fashion. They agree to let the young one go, even though it must remain in the crawler."

Kirk had no idea which gesticulations were indicative of pleasure among Lactrans, but it seemed certain that the youngster was performing some of them now.

He turned to communications. "Security, Lieutenant Uhura. I'll want Lieutenant Meyers to pilot the shuttlecrawler."

"Very well, Captain." Uhura moved to contact the crewman.

With the young Lactran aboard, the shuttlecrawler was loaded close to maximum. So much so that there was no room for the large, well-armed security team Kirk would have liked to take along—he hadn't forgotten the Lactrans' claim that the Boqus might seek to enforce their privacy. Instead, he had to count on the Lactrans' familiarity and former association with the race which now might still survive on the hidden surface.

The shuttlecrawler's descent to the coordinates plotted by Sulu and others was memorable, a welcome change from the convenience but monotony of the transporter. They soared down through an atmosphere structured like a cotton-candy parfait.

Its outermost layers were thick, rich orange and gray and pink. These colors gave way gradually to bright red-orange, then kilometers of raging maroon, then to a wholly unexpected layer of brilliant blue-green, which merged in its turn into a lavish red.

Eventually they emerged into a relatively clear layer above the surface and were able to look up at the sky as the Boqus saw it. Overhead rolled a thick collage of mauve cumulus, while hundreds of kilometers off to the south-southeast the threatening hemispheres of argent nimbus seemed to bubble and collapse like shiny balloons in a bucket of blood.

Kirk forgot their mission momentarily as he, Spock, and McCoy stared raptly at the silver storm. Sequential flashes of many-fingered lightning bolts deluged the surface with millions of volts.

Rising to meet the shuttlecrawler was a dimly visible landscape of orange and brown. The ground was pockmarked with deep pores filled with liquid ammonia. Kirk would do no swimming on this world. Lieutenant Meyers remained professionally oblivious to this beauty as he skillfully guided the craft down through unexpected blasts of hurricane-force wind.

Vegetation became identifiable as Lieutenant Meyers dropped them still lower. It was predominantly yellow and orange, with isolated patches of sparkling white.

Kirk thought he saw a multiple-limbed growth half as big as the *Enterprise* reflecting the light like a diamond and hinting of a composition other than cellulose.

Meyers spiraled in around the point plotted by Sulu. It was near the end of their approach that McCoy exclaimed in surprise and pointed forward.

Ahead lay a valley. One end was dominated by the glassy surface of a large lake of as yet unknown composition. The other was filled with an enormous fanlike artificial construction mounted on struts sufficient to make a millipede jealous. In the foreground was a city.

"Meyers?" Kirk inquired simply.

"Yes, sir. According to my coordinates, that should be the source of the light beam." Visual reconnaissance accomplished, he banked the awkward shuttlecrawler in the direction of the fan end of the valley. They began passing over the city, and the expectations suddenly raised so high vanished. Even the young Lactran appeared to droop.

Because it was dead. Dead as the hollow sockets of an old, bleached skull. Not that it was crumbling and broken like a hundred similar urban mausoleums Kirk had seen before. In fact, it looked remarkably well preserved. But nothing moved in its streets; no vehicles stirred between structures or above them. The silence below them was of the dead, or, at least, of the dying.

They flew on for a surprising distance over abandoned edifices, past towering spires and the gaping defunct domes resembling antique jewelry from which a patient thief had pried all the gems. As the city continued to unroll beneath them, Kirk began to sense its true size, and that of the fanlike structure they were nearing.

Almost as if in response to their filling spirits, a faint sign of life caught their attention, as well as that of the sensors.

From the far end of the valley, defining their destination, the light beam began to rise, this time but a feeble imitation, a shadow in light of the cloud-piercing shaft which had bathed the *Enterprise* in unexpected radiance. It barely rose above the valley, straining for an intensity apparently no longer attainable.

Once, twice, it flickered, the second time almost reaching to the lowest layer of orange clouds before dying.

But to those on board the shuttlecrawler, who had begun to give up hope, it was as encouraging as a neon sign the size of a Starfleet station. Meyers swung the shuttlecrawler lower, cutting speed as rapidly as he dared in the tricky, buffeting winds.

"Ask our friend," Kirk told Spock, "to see if he can sense any alien thoughts nearby." In contrast to this world, the young Lactran seemed welcomingly familiar.

There was a short pause, at the conclusion of which Spock informed them, "There is nothing, but I am told it does not matter. It is only what was expected. According to the records relevant to Boqu, they were never able to communicate mentally with the inhabitants over any distance. A Lactran, to touch the mind of a Boqus, would have to be in its actual presence."

Kirk refused to be discouraged. "Something caused that beam to be generated, whether the Lactrans can detect the mind behind it or not. Something that wanted to signal the *Enterprise* and a moment ago attempted to signal us."

"It could have been automatic, self-sustaining machinery, Captain," Spock pointed out coolly.

"Always encouraging, that's our Spock," declared McCoy with false gaiety. The shuttlecrawler rocked in a gust of hot orange wind, and he put out a hand to steady himself.

"I wish you would refrain from overutilization of the possessive form, Doctor," the first officer replied. "I was merely pointing out that—"

"Later, you two!" Kirk snapped. "Have a look at that." He pointed out the side port.

They were nearing the metallic fan, as peculiar a conglomeration as Kirk had ever set eyes on. It resembled the work of some careful colossus of a spider. Not that of a web spider, whose miniature marvels of engineering follow magnificently mathematical patterns, rather the simple cobwebs of the less precise arachnid, which throws and tosses its strands of silk with seeming abandon in any convenient corner, creating a less dignified though equally effective trap.

To the immediate right of this enormous arrangement of struts, beams, cables, and things Kirk couldn't name was a long, low building isolated from the nearest part of the city. Like the other structures they'd passed over, this one appeared relatively well maintained.

"Try to set down as close to that building as possible, Meyers," Kirk instructed.

"Yes, sir. I think there's enough clear space alongside."

As they commenced their final drop, Kirk gazed wonderingly at the huge construct. That it was the generator of the light beam he had no doubt. "It's not a mirror, Spock," he commented, "it has exactly the opposite of a smooth surface."

"According to the Lactrans," the first officer explained, "the peculiar light-metal and stone technology of the Boqus originated in a unique mind. The Lactrans do not find it unusual, therefore, that Boquian physics should find unique expression—"

"You can ask them yourself in a minute, Jim," McCoy broke in, settling himself tensely in his seat. "We're setting down."

Meyers made an admirable landing under difficult turbulence conditions. Once down, he engaged the ground engine, and the shuttlecrawler instantly became a vehicle for surface transport. They moved slowly toward the single large building near the fan construct.

Kirk saw that it was several stories high, with a gently curving roof. Totally devoid of windows or similar apertures, it appeared to be constructed of gray rock, though he did not doubt that on closer inspection the material might turn out to be something considerably more sophisticated. A race did not evolve and mature on a world like this, make contact successfully with an advanced people like the Lactrans, retain the technology capable of producing, even briefly, that atmosphere-slicing light beam, while building out of plain rock.

Gradually they neared the barnlike structure and began hunting along its edge for something that might be an entrance. They finally discovered one, facing the immense latticework of metal, which towered above them now like a forest of gigantic trees grown in free-fall and then transported to the planet's surface.

Kirk unstrapped himself and moved to the port, walking with considerable difficulty under the strong gravity. Beyond lay the vast enigmatic building, containing either aid for additional journeying or only a mechanical apologist for a dead civilization.

"I feel like I'm wearing lead boots," McCoy complained, fighting to keep from falling over under the increased gravity.

"At least we don't need armor suits, Bones," pointed out Kirk. "Be grateful for small favors."

"The only small favor I'll be grateful for is an indication we can return home," the doctor replied irritably, though his irritation was directed more at his own clumsiness in the one and a half g's than at the captain.

Like men drugged, Kirk, Spock, McCoy, and Meyers spent several long minutes moving experimentally about the cabin of the shuttlecrawler, trying to acclimate themselves to their increased weight. The young Lactran watched with interest. His strange physical configuration enabled him to move about with relative ease, though there were no signs that might be interpreted as amusement as he regarded the awkward movements of the men. Possibly, Kirk mused, the trip was having a maturing effect upon him.

"It regrets being unable to accompany us, Captain, but will be in constant communication with us through me as we explore the building. It expresses anxiety for our safety."

Kirk made an effort at effortlessness. "Tell it we'll

manage," he told Spock. "Life-support belts, gentle-men."

Each man donned one of the thick, self-contained belts which had long ago (excepting special situations) made the restrictive "space suits" of primitive times obsolete. Activation produced lime-yellow auras around them, whereupon they entered the lock of the shuttlecrawler and waited as machinery cycled the air and opened the outside door. Walking carefully but with increasing confidence, they moved down the ramp and found themselves standing on the densely packed, gravelly surface of Boqu.

"Anything from our young friend, Spock?"

"Nothing, Captain. He can sense nothing."

Kirk hadn't expected anything else. "Tell it to keep us informed of any change it can sense . . . and of any suggestions it comes up with as to how to proceed."

"Very well, Captain."

More than anything else, the featureless structure resembled an enormous warehouse, though Kirk doubted that was its actual function. It rose seamlessly above them and blended into the distant curving roof.

Directly before them what looked like several doors were recessed into the wall, scattered seemingly at random at various distances from one another.

"Might as well try the nearest one as any and go on from there," Kirk announced, his open communicator carrying his words to his companions.

Lightning flashed nearby as they began walking slowly toward the closest door. Spock's attention was still partially diverted by the giant jackstraw arrangement behind them. "A remarkable feat of engineering," he murmured. "The principles behind it imply a metallurgic technology radically different from our own. I wish I knew how it was built, let alone how it generates the radiance it does."

"Maybe the Boqus can tell you," advised McCoy, "if any are left."

They had reached the wall and stopped before the first recess. The door was of an unmistakably different composition from that of the structure's exterior, and had the look of machined metal. The recess was narrow at the top and quite wide at the base, rather like a pyramid with a domed crown, and rose to a height of two and a half meters.

"Indicative of heavy-gravity physiology," observed Spock easily.

"That's assuming this entrance is designed for the Boqus themselves," argued McCoy. "For all we know, this could be a local livestock barn. Maybe the Boqus were tall and spindly and just raised squatty cattle."

"Unlikely, Doctor," countered a disapproving Spock.

Attempts to open the door which formed the far wall of the niche met with failure. Attempts to open succeeding doors met with successive failures. Not only did none of them show signs of opening, they betrayed no hint of how they might be opened. Inspect as they might, the little party could find nothing resembling a handle, knob, keyhole, depression-response pit, or anything else they would have recognized.

Kirk was about to try a swift kick on the sixth and last door, a gesture which would have been not just futile but dangerous in the heavy gravity, when it slid aside smoothly. Life-belt sensors carried a thick whine to them as powerful machinery shifted the massive door, fighting its inertia.

"Automatics?" Meyers asked rhetorically, regarding the dim interior with a professional's eye.

"Maybe," murmured McCoy, "though despite my first impressions I've got to admit it looks more and more like we're expected. After you, Spock," he said, gesturing.

Once past the door (which, Kirk was gratified to see, showed no inclination to close suddenly behind them), they found themselves in a long trapezoidal hallway. At regular intervals its walls and ceilings were lined with panels phosphorescent with orange light. It bent and wound confusingly, but the distance covered was less than it seemed (the gravity wearing on them again) before they emerged into a vast, brightly lit chamber.

The roof arched overhead, and the surrounding

walls were filled with consoles and instrumentation as alien and unrecognizable as the material they were constructed of. Larger panels threw more light here, though it was still of that uniform orange hue. Kirk found the warm tint it lent to the metal furnishings very attractive, though it could never take the place of the familiar light of Earth's sun.

The greatest surprise, however, was not the instrumentation but the decor. On first glance, the chamber appeared to be lavishly landscaped, filled with strange bushes and small clusters of trees. McCoy had moved to feel the petals of a purple leafed growth, and drew back in surprise, apparently at the tactile sensation he received from the bush. For a fearful second Kirk thought the doctor had been stung.

"Are you hurt, Bones?"

"What? No, Jim, it's this thing." He glanced around at the other growths. "It's all of them, probably. The surface is cold . . . and hard. Hard as rock."

Kirk moved to stand alongside him, and regarded the construction. "Interesting . . . is it mineral sculpture, or what?"

Nearby, Spock was studying a taller specimen. "If so, Captain, the imitation is carried to remarkable extremes." He gestured at the base of the tree-thing, where it disappeared into the open earth. "It seems to enter the ground, obviously drawing support from it. I wonder if it may not draw more than that."

"Oh, come on, Spock! It's stone, or something equally inorganic. Obviously it—"

A friendly, oddly prickling thought appeared abruptly in McCoy's mind—in all their minds.

"Nothing is obvious, everything is infinitely indeterminate," the thought explained sharply. "You look intensely, physician, but not well."

Kirk spun and glanced around the chamber. It still appeared deserted. "Where are you," he asked warily, adding almost as an afterthought, "man of Boqu?"

"Closer than you think, Captain Kirk."

One of the "trees" nearby started toward them.

Kirk found himself face to . . . well, to something,

with one of the strangest creatures he had ever seen. By comparison, the bulky, limbless Lactrans appeared almost normal.

The being moved on a base two meters across, consisting of hundreds of long dark yellow limbs. Stiff and many-jointed, they rippled with an eerie clacking along the hard floor, like the march of millions of ants on a sheet of paper.

The centilimbs radiated from a thick central post twice as broad as a man's body, roughly circular in form, like an addled fence post. This main part was shaded a deep brown, almost the color of unpolished mahogany, and was veined with exterior vertical ribs of gold.

It rose in three jointed sections to the level of Kirk's nose, then tapered slightly before spreading out into a wide circular plate whose upper surface was plano-convex, like the upper half of the *Enterprise*'s primary hull.

The head, or such Kirk considered it, was a milky opaque crystalline substance resembling rutilated quartz. Black striations ran through it, bunching into dark nodules at various points within.

From the flat underside of the head, set several centimeters in from the fringe, dangled long articulated tentacles of dark yellow. They were similar in shape and form to the hundreds of skittering feet projecting from the Boqus's base. They swayed and moved easily, under obvious control.

It was impossible to tell whether the expedition was facing the creature's front, back, or side, or indeed if such terms meant anything in regard to a Boqus. Equally, there was nothing faintly identifiable as a mouth, nose, eyes, ears, or anything else indicative of a face.

Kirk elected to regard the portion of the being facing him as its front. "I'm—" He cleared his throat, still recovering from the initial surprise of the Boqus's unmasking. "I am Captain James T. Kirk of the U.S.S. *Enterprise*. This is my first officer, Mr. Spock; my chief medical officer, Dr. McCoy; and sec—our vehicle pilot, Lieutenant Meyers."

This produced an agitated jangling of those dangling tentacles, and the creature seemed to draw back. Could he have made a mistake already, Kirk mused?

He had not. "Chief medical officer!" came the excited thought. "Then you have come in response to the prayers of the *animax!*"

"Prayers? Animax?" McCoy echoed in confusion. The Boqus's limbs relaxed, but its thoughts were still in turmoil.

"You have not come in response to our need, to end the epidemic?"

Kirk suddenly understood the reason behind the deserted metropolis they had passed over, and felt saddened as McCoy replied, "I'm truly sorry. We know nothing of any local epidemic."

The Boqus appeared to slump, and the opaqueness in its crystal skull increased until the striations within could no longer be seen.

"Why then," it inquired with sudden brisk curiosity, "have you come here? I cannot believe it was by accident."

That Kirk could sympathize with. Boqu was not a world the casual explorer would stumble upon. "We are here at the request of an ancient race acquainted with your people," he explained, "the people of Lactra."

"Lactra, Lactra," the uncertain thought reached them. "I know them not. I am old, visitors, yet this is something well past my forming. Admitted it is that we Boqus are sadly lacking in methods of history and social record. We follow our past not as well as we ought to."

The suspicions brewing in McCoy's mind, temporarily interrupted when the Boqus had revealed himself, now surged back full strength, not to be denied.

"Jim, these bushes and trees around us—the Boqus himself—Spock's hesitation in classifying them was justified. They're not sculptured any more than you or I are sculptured." He rushed on, flushed with excitement. "We've long postulated the possibility of a living organism based on the silicon atom instead of carbon. Boqu . . . Boqu is a whole world based on that substance. A world of living crystal."

"I sense carefully concealed distaste in your mind, physician," came the thought from the creature before them. "Pity us not. It is we who have always been sorry for those we know of you. You poor carbon-based creatures, with your saggy, flexible, unrigid limbs. Your bodies lack discipline and form and true beauty.

"Even so, for all our inherent superior endurance to disease, we are not immune, it seems." The thought seemed to brighten in Kirk's mind, brighten with uncertain hope. "It is true you are a medical scientist, Bones McCoy?"

"I'm a doctor," McCoy replied readily. "My job's to make sick people unsick."

"Concise, yet thorough enough," came the response. "A great epidemic of tragic proportions has ravaged Boqu for many *nevars*. It is conceded among the surviving scientists that a new approach to a solution is required. We had despaired of ever finding one. Yet here you are."

"Now just a minute," began a cautious McCoy, but the Boqus rambled on.

"If you could find a cure for this devastation, you would gain the eternal gratitude of all the people of my world." Many limbs moved, indicating all directions simultaneously. "This is but one of many laboratories scattered about the surface of Boqu, isolated to protect those surviving scientists while they exhaust every means in the search for a solution. I was granted the opportunity of watching for an unlikely savior from afar. It was I who signaled you with the light, and it was you who responded. I solicit your aid."

Everyone, it seemed, needed their help, Kirk thought. McCoy returned to his protest.

"I don't know how to cure a sick rock. I don't know the first thing about silicon biology."

"No one does, Doctor," pointed out Spock, "since

until this moment such a thing was not thought to exist."

"However," McCoy added reluctantly, at the overpowering sense of desolation the Boqus projected, "I'm willing to try."

"No more than that could be asked," replied the Boqus ringingly. "I am Hivar the Toq, and will aid you ..." The thought faded, to be unexpectedly replaced by a mental frown of contrition. "But you are here for another reason, at the request of these beings you call Lactrans. I cannot interfere with prior obligations."

"I don't think it will matter," Kirk informed him. "Matter of fact, the Lactrans are here to ask for *your* help."

"Poor help we can give now, for anything," Hivar the Toq confessed. "Yet I would hear the circumstances."

"The Lactrans," Kirk explained, "have made much of their world over into a great zoo, a collection of diverse life forms the inspection of which provides them with knowledge and pleasure. They wish to add one last creature to this assemblage, one creature they have failed to capture over the centuries. We were told that only your people possess the means to capture such a being, which they call a jawanda."

Hivar considered for a moment, its mind intent on unscrambling this new riddle.

"The creature your friends call the jawanda troubled Boqu for many *multinevars*," it finally informed them. "We have not had the need to control them since then, for they have learned to avoid us. Yet I have some knowledge of the means you speak of."

Kirk glanced to Spock, then McCoy. The Lactrans had been reluctant to divulge details of the jawanda, for reasons unknown. Perhaps true ignorance was the honest one; possibly the evasion was intentional. Regardless, Hivar the Toq apparently knew of the creatures. At the moment they were in mental contact with the young Lactran, but out of immediate danger of Lactran attack. If there was a serious reason for this concealment of facts ...

Kirk made his decision and asked hastily, "We're still not too sure what a jawanda is. If you could explain..."

No mental blast sent him writhing to the floor, but the Boqus didn't respond with an answer, either.

'I will bargain with you, Captain Kirk," Hivar announced, scuttling in small circles, "and with your friends of Lactra." Several crystalline tentacles pointed sharply at McCoy. "If your medical scientist Bones McCoy can discover a cure for the disease which plagues my people, then I will consult with the surviving guardians of the trust of science to see what can be done about the jawanda."

"Listen," McCoy objected, "I said I'd be willing to try. But I've no experience. Making our journey's success contingent upon my solving something which hasn't even been imagined until now just isn't fair."

"Somehow you must do more than try, medical scientist."

Kirk had the impression of a stone back being turned to them.

"Whatever you need will be provided instantly. We can expect no other visitors, for our signals have gone unheeded. Your presence is proof of that, since you are not here in response to them. We can expect no help beyond your own."

"How can you expect me, someone totally ignorant of your body chemistry, your very makeup, to succeed where your own best scientists have failed?" an exasperated McCoy wanted to know.

Hivar the Toq replied almost sullenly. "I do not know myself. I know only that a new approach offers the best remaining chance of a solution. Your very ignorance saves you from the misconceptions and false approaches which have stifled us."

"First time anyone ever complimented me for ignorance," McCoy grumbled. "I've got to forget four thousand years of biology and start from scratch."

"Does that mean you're convinced you can't do it, Bones?" wondered a concerned Kirk.

McCoy shook his head. "No. It means I'd better get

started. Let's see ... I'm going to need Nurse Chapel, and Ensigns M'baww and Prox to help with the beginning research, certain equipment ... and I'm sure the Lactrans will have suggestions and instruments I'll have to learn about."

Kirk was studying the equipment set in consoles and banks throughout the chamber. "There's plenty to keep the rest of us occupied in the meantime, Bones. I don't think the Boquses will object to answering a few questions."

"We do not, Captain Kirk," Hivar the Toq admitted softly, "so long as there are any of us left to answer."

VIII

With the aid of Hivar and information relayed from various centers of research on Boqu, McCoy made progress which surprised him. It took two weeks to understand what the result of the disease was.

"I know what's happening to the Boqus now, Jim," he explained, "but as to the cause, I've no more idea than they do." He gazed helplessly around the small medical lab which had been set up in the shuttlecrawler, enabling him to work outside the constraints of a life-support belt.

He gestured toward a table laden with slides and instruments. It reminded Kirk of something familiar, yet elusive. His attention was taken by McCoy.

"Something is causing an alteration in the structure of the Boqus' upper parts, changing the chemical composition in such a way that death is inevitable. Imagine the blood in your veins suddenly petrifying and you'll have some idea of what's happening to Hivar and the others.

"I've spent days hunting for a way to attack this thing and, Jim, I don't have the faintest notion of how to begin. This is as alien to my experience as we are to the Boqus."

"I have a suggestion, Doctor McCoy," came a prickling inside their heads.

"Who's that, Spock?" Kirk asked.

"One of the Boquian scientists who has traveled many *nevars* to reach here," the first officer explained. "It has been observing us at work and has considered the situation. Our presence—our very existence—has given it an idea it wishes to propose."

"I'm all . . . whatever it is I'm supposed to listen with," McCoy announced.

"There is no need to tense, Doctor," soothed Spock. "The idea has been communicated to me to relay to you. It is suggested that since your function is the study and treatment of carbon-based forms, you consult with one of the many on board the *Enterprise* who are experts in compounds of silicon."

"Spock," Kirk began, "we've already explained to them that life based on silicon instead of carbon is unknown—was unknown—to us until we came here. We have no one who—"

"Of course!" McCoy blurted unexpectedly. He ignored first Kirk's stare, then his query, as he hurried to the forward intercom. *"Enterprise, Enterprise!"* When no reply was immediately forthcoming, he stared angrily at the console. "Now what's the matter? Don't our maintainance techs realize that delays . . . !"

Spock quietly activated the communications unit for him and stood aside.

This time McCoy's entreaties were rewarded with a flood of static, as the communicator strove to force its way through dense atmosphere and the barrage of internal Boquian radiation.

"Enterprise, Lieutenant Uhura speaking. Is that you, Dr. McCoy?"

"Yes, Uhura. I want to speak to Lieutenant K'ang Te." He glanced at Spock as if for confirmation, and the first officer nodded readily.

Kirk searched his memory for one name out of the

hundreds on board the *Enterprise*. K'ang Te, lieutenant; Sciences; head of the geology section.

Then he wondered why he hadn't thought of it. It had been a Boqus's turn to find a different approach . . .

With the veteran mineralogist's assistance, McCoy began to make progress—man and woman, physician and geologist, working together in search of a solution. Kirk watched them drive themselves mercilessly and wondered worriedly which they would find first—an answer, or total exhaustion.

It appeared to Kirk to be a dead heat between the two possibilities when McCoy, drawn from the work and the debilitating affect of hard labor under an extra half gravity, staggered onto the bridge a week and a day later.

"Bones, you look terrible!" Kirk exclaimed.

"I know. And I feel wonderful!"

"You—you did it, then? You actually found a solution?"

"K'ang Te and I, yes . . . At least, we think so."

Kirk looked past him. "Where is the lieutenant?"

"In Sick Bay, where I sent her." A hint of a smile graced the doctor's dry lips. "It's easy to prescribe treatment for someone when you're suffering the same symptoms." He sank gratefully into a seat vacated by Spock, too tired to counter the gesture with sarcasm—or too thankful for the small courtesy.

"I am certain the solution is as fascinating as the disease, Doctor," Spock ventured, by way of impelling McCoy to explanation.

"You don't know the tenth of it, Spock. The trouble was with their circulatory system—you ought to see it, Jim! Their blood, if we can call it that, is thicker than machine oil, and flows just fast enough to be called something better than paralyzed. In past centuries certain crucial components within the blood haven't been breaking down as they should have. Call it a buildup of impurities, if you will. The Boqus thought something in their own systems responsible for handling the breakdown of these impurities had failed, and they've been going slowly insane trying to discover it. We found it, but the real problem was finding an antidote." He shook his head slowly. "The Boqus were too close to the problem."

"As so often happens," Spock finished for him. "I am intriguied, Doctor. What kind of remedy did you discover capable of affecting the buildup of unwanted substances in the 'blood' of a silicon-based creature?"

"To begin with, Spock, I had to disregard, throw out, forget, and otherwise ignore everything I knew about serums and standard antidote chemistry. Not only did it seem unlikely I'd be able to find something the Boquian researchers had missed, but I wouldn't have the faintest idea of how to go about inoculating a rock—for all its stiffly formal mobility, I can't help thinking of Hivar and its kind in those terms. Our eventual solution came from medicine by way of physics, born out of mineralogy." He settled himself into a chair, lowering himself gently.

"According to their meteorological records, Boqu is periodically afflicted with long periods of constant storm. We nearly hit one of them on our way down— remember the tremendous lightning display?"

Both Kirk and Spock recalled that casually awesome discharge of energy clearly.

"After more experimentation and search than I care to think about, we discovered that in the case of this last series of storms, the cloud layer over most of inhabited Boqu had become so thick as to block out certain radiations from the system's feeble sun. This was accomplished by having Astrophysics prepare a complete breakdown of the radiation the sun was putting out, and comparing it with readings taken on the surface. From that point, we had to proceed with special caution. One of those screened-out wavelengths might be responsible for breaking down the unwanted substances in the Boqus' blood—but the others might prove lethal if too strong a dose was delivered."

He sighed slowly. "As it turned out, nothing of the sort happened, though that didn't keep all involved from worrying constantly about it. We tried four different radiants on several fatally ill Boqus. Two did nothing, the third made the experimental subject retch remarkably, and the fourth—the fourth had its subject on its, uh, feet in a few hours. Similar radiation treatments ought to have most of Boqu back to normal inside a month. The equipment involved is simple to reproduce. A technical team is on the surface now, helping them set up facilities for duplicating the proper projectors."

"Fascinating, Doctor," commented Spock with admiration. "I would enjoy a more detailed look into such a unique physiology."

McCoy's expression turned solemn. "That shouldn't be too hard a wish to fulfill, Spock. At present Boqu enjoys a surplus of corpses. They'd probably find the dissection of a Vulcan cadaver equally interesting."

"Undoubtedly," agreed the first officer, missing the irony of the doctor's statement completely.

Unexpectedly, McCoy grinned. He leaned his head on his left hand as he reminisced. "I don't think we'll ever see a Boqus jump. They're not constructed for leaping. But, Jim, when that last patient suddenly showed signs of recovery and we knew we'd found the answer, Hivar and the Boqus medical scientists present came as near to kicking up their heels as their bodies permit."

"How long does the treatment last?" Kirk wanted to know.

McCoy considered. "Only about one of our weeks. So until the intensity of this severe storm cycle begins to lessen, every Boqus will have to spend about fifteen minutes a week under a radiation projector in order for its blood to return to normal—like humans used to do under sun lamps."

Spock looked querulous. " 'Sun lamp,' Captain?"

"An old obsession of people in the Dark Ages, Mr. Spock. Many of them used to spend hours, even days, under the concentrated radiation of an ultraviolet generator, trying to artificially darken their skin."

The first officer's confused expression did not fade. "I see, Captain. But I was under the impression that during that period of human history the humans with light-toned skin discriminated against the darker humans."

"That's right, Spock," Kirk admitted.

Spock's puzzlement deepened. "Then why would the light-skinned humans try to burn their skin dark? This is not logical, Captain."

"Human actions of the Dark Ages rarely were, Spock. As a matter of fact, I seem to recall that certain humans of dark skin used artificial means to try to lighten their skin."

"So the light-skinned humans tried to make their skins dark, and some of the dark-skinned humans tried to make theirs light?"

"You've got it, Spock."

The first officer assumed an air of finality. "I will never understand human beings fully, Captain."

"Don't worry about it, Spock," advised McCoy, for once in complete agreement with him, "you've got plenty of company. Actually, if you bother to consider that . . ." He stopped in mid-sentence, aware that the first officer was no longer listening. Instead, Spock's mind was drawn to something deeper.

"It is the Lactrans, Captain," he finally declared, confirming what the watching Kirk and McCoy had already suspected. "Though growing impatient, they applaud Dr. McCoy's ability and great talent in finding a solution to the Boquian epidemic."

"It's not a question of talent," an embarrassed McCoy muttered, "just persistence."

"I have so informed them," Spock added drily. "They wish to know if we have made inquiries among the Boqus for their help in locating and capturing a jawanda."

"They can ask our hosts themselves shortly." Kirk thumbed a switch on the chair arm, activating the intercom.

"Engineering," a familiar voice acknowledged.

"Scotty, this is the captain. How is that special tech section coming on those big life-support belts for the Lactrans?"

"I was about to call in myself, sir," the chief engineer told him. "They're undergoin' final tests. I think our guests will be pleased with them. No need to use the shuttlecrawler any more. It wasn't too difficult a job—even for us 'primitive types.' Just time-consumin'. They can even take 'em off and put 'em on themselves, with those flexible snouts of theirs."

"Thank you, Scotty. Kirk out." He turned back to the motionless Spock. "You can tell our friends they can describe jawanda-catching requirements to Hivar the Toq in person. Mr. Scott's people have built three specially modified life-support belts for them. They can beam down to the surface with us."

When they beamed down that afternoon, Kirk saw hints of tremendous activity in the direction of the formerly moribund city. On the nearest outskirts, crews of rejuvenated Boqus were at work in incomprehensible machinery, modifying certain structures, demolishing others, building still more.

Obviously, McCoy's antidote was already having extensive effects. Certainly, the captain thought as they made their way cautiously through the heavy gravity of Boqu, Hivar and its colleagues should now be overjoyed enough to provide all the aid the Lactrans desired.

Those three massive aliens were sliding along smoothly behind Kirk, Spock, and McCoy. The captain envied them their ease of locomotion in the Boquian gravity.

At the moment they were deep in conversation among themselves, long front ends bobbing and weaving as they conversed at a speed which to human minds was only a confusing, head-throbbing blur. Enormous lightning flashes arced from thick clouds to ground off to the north.

"What are they so intent on, Mr. Spock?" his curiosity finally prompted him to ask. "The electrical display?"

"No, Captain." Kirk forced his way through thick, clinging mud that wasn't there. "The laboratory structure of Hivar the Toq." Kirk gazed at it, but saw nothing remarkable about the large building save its lack of windows.

"What about it intrigues them so?"

"The acuteness of its construction, Captain. It is all sharp angles and abutments, excepting the roof, whereas Lactran architecture is based on an absence of sharpness. Their buildings and machines, if you recall our stay on Lactra, were all rounded—curves, ovoids, hemispheres and circles. It seems that structure follows form. The Lactrans are as rounded as their constructs, the Boqus as sharp-edged as theirs."

"And what about us?" asked McCoy curiously. Spock paused a moment.

"We are considered acute formations by the Lactrans and curvilinear by the Boqus. It seems we partake of something of both."

"So we're mediators in form as well as in fact," noted Kirk. "It's nice to be consistent."

This time the last door of reflective metal was open, awaiting their arrival. Scott probably could have beamed them directly into the central chamber, but Kirk wanted Hivar to have time to prepare for their arrival—and it might prove useful to discover if the Lactrans could negotiate the building's passageways.

Nothing of the irritability mentioned in the Lactrans' old records was evident in the manner of Hivar the Toq as it greeted them warmly. The Lactrans studied the instrumentation and the layout of the circular laboratory with admiration.

The Boquian scientist had been taking McCoy's radiation treatments, and the change in its appearance was dramatic. The gold ribbing on its central trunk shone as if polished, Kirk observed immediately.

Even more striking was the difference in Hivar's upper region, the part that Kirk had come to think of as a head. Except for a few isolated patches of color, the opaque milkiness which had characterized that hemispheric crystalline structure on their first meeting was gone. Now the dark internal striations and peculiar clumps and nodes of denser material showed clearly, reminding Kirk of ferns and flies frozen in Earth's ancient amber.

It was a measure of this creature's personal strength, Kirk realized suddenly, that in all this time since their initial meeting Hivar had never once indicated that it too was severely stricken with radiation deficiency. Kirk wondered if he could have remained as personally unconcerned if their positions had been reversed—if he had been the one dying of a disease thought incurable and Hivar the possible savior.

"Greetings, Captain Kirk, Mr. Spock, Doctor Bones McCoy." Kirk had the impression the Boqus was glancing behind them, though, try as he might, he could not identify Hivar's organs of sight. "And anxious visitors from our far past." Something scratched at Kirk's mind as the Lactrans and the Boqus exchanged silent mental hellos.

When it continued, he wondered for a nervous moment if something had gone wrong, if the Lactrans had touched some ancient trouble. Spock reassured him.

"According to the youngster, its parents and Hivar are engaged in parallel telepathic conversation of an advanced mode. I can believe that, as I have tried to listen in and have experienced only a mild mental concussion as a result. While the Lactrans must turn their thoughts to baby talk and slow their conceptualizations to a crawl in order for us to comprehend, no such restriction exists between them and the Boqus."

Whether Hivar the Toq sensed Kirk's uneasiness at being so completely left out of what was obviously a critical discussion or was just being polite, Kirk would never know. In any case, he appreciated it with loud thoughts of thanks when the Boqus slowed its own river of conversation enough for the humans to make some sense of it.

"A jawanda you want to capture and take back with you to your home world? A jawanda!"

The Boqus' expression of surprise, coming when they had expected a more casual acknowledgment, left the humans startled.

"Now listen," McCoy began, "we've been put off

about this jawanda long enough. I think it's about time we—"

Hivar the Toq pivoted on centilegs, the gesture of turning away from them more significant than anything else. "I promised you our aid, it is true, but ... I do not know." It was muttering mentally. "Long ago we had a device for manipulating the jawandas. But this was used only to protect Boqu, to drive the creatures away from our world. Never to capture one!"

"Just a second, Hivar," McCoy interrupted, waving his hands. "Let's back up a minute. You said drive them *away* from *Boqu?*" The doctor eyed Kirk uncertainly, and was rewarded by a cautioning look of equal puzzlement. "Aren't the jawandas native to Boqu? Are you trying to tell us they originate on still another world?"

"None of the other planets of the system appeared capable of supporting even rudimentary life," Spock commented, without committing himself utterly. Perhaps some minor error in their initial hurried observations, some small factor of atmosphere overlooked ...

"Do not tax yourself, friend Spock," came the answering thought from Hivar the Toq—accompanied, Kirk sensed with surprise, by a twinge of amusement. "It would appear that your friends the Lactrans have been less than informative, Captain Kirk."

Kirk turned his gaze on the always silent aliens. The answer to his unvoiced question came, as usual, from Spock.

"No, Captain, they have told us no untruths, they have not lied to us. They have simply neglected to mention certain details concerning the jawandas."

"I can imagine!" exclaimed McCoy feelingly.

"It is these details which they have not supplied which should be of particular interest to you, Captain," Hivar added helpfully. "I have said that we manipulated the jawandas out of necessity, to keep them clear of our world. This does not mean they come from another. We have never been able to determine the origin of the jawandas—if, indeed, such a term has application in their case. We know only where the jawandas exist ... out there." Half a dozen reticulate upper tentacles pointed jerkily skyward.

"The jawanda is truly a creature of the universe," Hivar explained to a rapt audience of bipeds. "They live only in intergalactic space, drifting for unknowable eons in the gulf between galaxies. We know very little of their life, save that they are simple yet marvelously efficient energy-mass converters, feeding on the faint radiations extant in the vast Out There."

"If these creatures exist on radiation," Spock inquired, "why remain in the comparative barrens of intergalactic territory? Why do they not come nearer the galaxies themselves, and the suns which produce the radiations on which they feed?"

"Gravity," was the terse explanation. "Should a jawanda come within the influence of a modest sun, it could easily be trapped forever in orbit about it. While there is no reason for assuming that a jawanda could not live, even thrive, in such a confined existence, it seems that they prefer freedom to satiety. It may be a survival instinct or an actual mental preference—we likely shall never know. For whatever reason, they avoid the gravitational density of galaxies and star clusters. Only the isolation and weak pull of our star made them bold enough to come near Boqu."

"Why Boqu, though?" asked McCoy.

"Remember our measurements on approach, Doctor," Spock reminded him. "Boqu puts out more radiation than it absorbs, qualifying it in certain astronomical lexicons as a protostar itself."

"Correct, Mr. Spock," the Boquian scientist concurred. "Jawandas used to frolic freely about our world, successfully defying our sun's poor gravity. Normally, this troubled Boqu not at all. The jawandas' absorption of radiation lost freely to space did not affect us.

"Occasionally, however, it did, according to the old records. No, Dr. McCoy, the question I see framed in your mind is reasonable but not relevant. The jawandas did not screen out any particular radiation from our sun—such as the vital one you isolated as the cause of our epidemic. Instead, they blocked out a majority of radiation, that wavelength included. More important than any disease, this unpredictable screening caused slight but disconcerting shifts in the surface temperature of Boqu, lowering the warmth in the regions affected by substantial amounts."

"I can see where it could be uncomfortable to be enjoying warm weather one minute and have it turn to winter in a few seconds," Kirk admitted readily.

"This situation persisted for thousands of our years," Hivar continued, "until we found a way to drag the jawandas away. While doubtless they are dull, thoughtless creatures, they do seem capable of learning through repetition. They learned long ago not to approach Boqu."

Hivar abruptly went silent, and Kirk and McCoy looked to the attentive Spock. "The Lactrans wonder what has become of the mechanism for manipulating the jawandas and whether it can be adapted to serve their needs. Hivar has replied that it can conceive of no reason why the device should not be so utilized, though it has never been done before. The Boqus wished to drive the jawandas away, not capture them."

"I do not even know if the mechanism still exists, and, if so, whether it remains operative," Hivar broadcast mentally, slowed now so that the intensely curious humans could also listen in. "Should it prove so, you may employ it, though this must be done with care. Certain of the extended components of the mechanism hold a historical attraction for us. We would not wish to see them lost."

"What components?" Kirk wanted to know.

That great crystalline head turned toward him. "Boqu is circled by nine moons, Captain Kirk. For manipulating the jawandas properly it is necessary to make use of six of them."

"Six . . . moons." McCoy gulped, turning to the *Enterprise*'s first officer. "How big did they say one of these creatures is?"

"It has not been stated, Doctor. All references to size have been of an indeterminate nature."

"Big enough to live in intergalactic space, Bones,"

Kirk commented slowly. "Big enough to pass between sun and planet and cause climatic changes on the surface. Big enough to . . ." His voice trailed off, and he turned to face the Lactrans. "We gave our word to help. That agreement stands." He directed his final statement to Hivar. "Find the device. Can it be mounted on the *Enterprise,* or does it too have to exist in free space?"

"No, Captain Kirk," the Boqus replied, bowing with surprising grace for so nearly inflexible a creature. "The actual console for controlling the confining elements of the mechanism is quite small. It will fit easily on board your vessel. As will I."

"You?" McCoy gaped at the scientist. "You're coming along?" Impressions of a mental nod of assent. "But why? You don't owe the Lactrans anything."

"Your guests, no . . . but you, Doctor McCoy, are owed a great deal. In any case, it is necessary, since only a Boqus could properly operate the mechanism."

The mysterious control console of the capture device turned out to be something of an anticlimax. Kirk had been prepared to have technicians cut out bulkheads and even cabins surrounding the Shuttlecraft Bay in order to provide a space large enough to accommodate a monstrous construction. As it turned out, the actual instrumentation bulked only about three times the size of the *Enterprise*'s navigation console. Hivar had found it in the nearby city housed in a huge old scientific warehouse that looked brand new, a testament to the foresight and talent of Boqu's pioneering engineers.

Hivar activated the ancient machine and spent several days replacing certain components and realigning internal components while Kirk fidgeted nervously on board the *Enterprise,* his sleep troubled by snaggletoothed apparitions bigger than starships.

When, before long, the renovation was complete, Kirk inspected the incredibly dense machine and ordered the bracing beneath a bulk-cargo transporter reinforced before beaming the device aboard. He was trying to imagine where they could conveniently place the machine—and how—when Spock proposed a solution so simple that Kirk had overlooked it.

"Why trouble to move it anywhere, Captain? Leave it where it is, on the transporter platform. If the Boqus can operate it from here, there's really no reason to shove it around the ship."

"How about communication?" Kirk mused, studying the distance between the transporter platform and the nearest intercom unit.

His first officer considered. "We will request that the young Lactran remain here with Hivar," he finally suggested. "The youngster will be in constant communication with its parents and with myself, on the bridge, as well as with Hivar."

"Boqus to Lactran to Vulcan," Kirk concluded, adding with firmness, "We'll keep all intercoms activated and open anyway."

When finally beamed aboard with the mechanism, Hivar reactivated it and pronounced itself satisfied with the arrangements. Pressed for a more precise translation than "mechanism" or "device," the Boqus scientist confessed it was unable to name it any better for his human hosts.

"At least that's in keeping with its appearance," Kirk murmured, staring at the object in question. It looked like a large blob of free-form slag composed of half a hundred materials, metallic and otherwise.

He studied the bumps and spikes and wires sticking out of the amorphous mass, trying to rationalize the haphazard appearance of the thing with the knowledge that it was an intricate, complex feat of alien engineering. There was slight consolation in the fact that it looked as absurd to the lumpish Lactrans as it did to him.

Duplicating the outward form of the thing would be no trouble, Kirk thought. Simply take a room full of engineering components and turn a low-power construction phaser on it. Several hours later you would have produced a close approximation of the object now squatting on the cargo-transporter platform.

As Hivar the Toq moved reflecting limbs across the mound's surface, however, it generated lights and hums and whines no half-welded dollop of metal could ever produce.

"The mechanism," the Boqus told them, "contains its own power source, which in turn links it with the much more powerful old engines locked into the crusts of the moons Drasid, Mett One and Mett Two, Lethiq, Lathoq, and Oj." It completed a few final adjustments, turned with a crystalline flourish to face them.

"All is in readiness, Captain Kirk."

An awkward moment of uncertainty followed, before Kirk finally replied, "You'll have to tell us how to begin." He glanced at the young Lactran, who showed no sign of providing instructions or suggestions. "No one else on board has any idea where to start looking for a jawanda."

"I expect your vessel possesses adequate equipment for the transmission of sound waves, since this is the method you use for personal communication," Hivar ventured. "Do you also have the ability to detect other types of electromagnetic radiation?"

"With considerable accuracy," Kirk informed it.

"Then there is no difficulty. Instruct your monitors of the appropriate instrumentation to listen for"—and Hivar provided a figure Spock understood—"which is the range of the jawandas' cry."

"Interesting," the first officer commented. "They communicate among themselves, then?"

"So it is believed by many," the Boqus acknowledged, "yet these sounds may be produced for a variety of reasons having little or nothing to do with communication. Should we continue outward from Boqu, away from the galaxy, we will eventually encounter one." A pause; then: "I see your confusion, Captain Kirk. Given the density of our atmosphere, how is it our knowledge of astronomy is so advanced? Let me say simply that our progress in what you might call radio astronomy and related areas which do not require visual observation has been substantial."

"That wasn't really what was bothering me," responded Kirk. "It was your use of the term 'eventually.' How long is eventually?"

Hivar transmitted a mental shrug. "It could be tomorrow . . . or it might be a hundred years. I would tend toward the former."

"I sincerely hope you're right," declared Kirk with feeling.

Once back on the bridge, Kirk's first concern was that the complex telepathic communications system—which, after all, relied on an adolescent of an alien species—was functioning smoothly.

"Mr. Spock, what's the maximum acceleration Hivar's mechanism can match?"

Again the relaxation into semistupor, which no longer troubled Kirk; then the first officer replied, "Warp-three, Captain. Should we attempt to travel any faster, the six moons which form the bulk of the system will fall behind, soon to be lost to control."

Kirk nodded and glanced at the helm. "All ahead warp-three, Mr. Sulu."

"Ahead warp-three," came the acknowledgment. It was followed by a hesitant question: "On what course, sir?"

Kirk looked expectantly at Spock, who informed him, "Hivar says to use your own judgment, Captain. One course should prove as efficacious as the next, so long as we continue to move outward from our galaxy."

"Um. Mr. Sulu, resume our former course heading, continuing on out from Boqu."

"Aye, Captain," the helmsman replied unquestioningly.

Kirk's gaze went to the main viewscreen. It provided an expansive panorama of obsidian emptiness, speckled fretfully with the pale light of far-off galaxies and star clusters hundreds of thousands and millions of light-years distant.

Given the *Enterprise*'s marvelous instrumentation, of course, it was next to impossible for them to become lost. Even so, one could not be certain of anything this far from familiar starmarks. The idea of becoming lost in this benumbing nothingness, to wander forever on the fringes of the galaxy, was an eventuality he had no wish to cope with. Resolutely, the captain forced it from his mind.

There were other things to think about. Like the actual size of the mysterious jawanda, for example.

"Activate rear scanners, Mr. Arex," he ordered. The depressing view ahead was temporarily replaced by a shrinking Boqu aft. Raging upper-atmospheric disturbances stirred orange-and-maroon clouds like a giant's finger dipped in paint. And there was something else.

Six points of darkness, artificially highlighted by the ship's scanner-computers, were following them at a respectful distance. Six moons, detached from orbit, trailed the *Enterprise* like balls on a string. Kirk assumed that the long line was for convenience of manipulation. Surely the actual use of the moons in jawanda capture involved some more-complex configuration.

The lift doors slid aside, and McCoy strolled onto the bridge. "You'll be happy to know, Jim, that Lieutenant Randolph is fully recovered. I discharged her from Sick Bay an hour ago." His gaze went to the screen. "Our six attendant satellites?" Kirk nodded.

"I hope Hivar knows what it's doing with that archaic hunk of machinery." McCoy gestured at the trailing moons. "Even if they are all smaller than Luna, I'd hate for Hivar to make one of them zig when it should zag. If the *Enterprise* accidentally got caught between them, we'd end up looking about as streamlined as a Lactran."

IX

On the sixth day out from Boqu, Lieutenant Uhura turned from her communications console and informed

Kirk, "I am receiving broadcasts in the range indicated by the Boquian scientist, Captain."

"You're certain, Lieutenant?"

"Yes, sir. Pickup is clearly within the frequency specified."

"Mr. Arex, obtain a fix on the broadcast source. As soon as you have it placed, instruct Mr. Sulu on the necessary alteration in our course for planned intercept."

"Very well, sir," the Edoan navigator replied.

Kirk glanced back at Uhura, intending to thank her—and hesitated. The lieutenant was chewing her lower lip, and she looked more than simply thoughtful.

"Something the matter, Uhura?"

"I don't think so, sir. It's just that . . . well, I'm sure I recognize those sounds. I've heard them before."

"That hardly seems likely, Lieutenant," commented Spock.

"I know, Mr. Spock," she admitted, "but I'm still positive I've encountered these particular noises in the past—or at least sounds very similar."

"Amplify and put them on the bridge speakers," Kirk decided.

She spent a moment adjusting the controls; then the bridge was filled with a moderate crackling sound. It alternated occasionally with a regular electronic chirp, which devolved rapidly into a low buzzing. One moment it sounded like random noise, the next almost like a programmed broadcast.

"My apology to Lieutenant Uhura," Spock finally said into the silence. "I recognize the sounds myself." Kirk was about to add that he also was familiar with such noise when Spock added, "I have communicated our discovery to Hivar, who is anxious to hear it."

"By all means. Uhura, transmit to the Bulk Transporter Room the Boqus is located in." There was a long wait.

"It is the cry of a jawanda," Spock announced, Hivar's own conviction mirrored in the first officer's tone.

Kirk was only confused further. "But that's a familiar sound, Mr. Spock. Large radiotelescopes, even the oldest ones on Earth, have been picking up buzzes and crackles like this one for hundreds of years. Of course," he added softly, "there are many whose origin has remained a mystery."

"Certain of those unsolved origins may now be explained, it seems," Spock went on, showing excitement of an intellectual sort even in his role of communicator. "It appears that in addition to quasars, pulsars, radio nebulae, and other known phenomena which are sources of deep-space radio waves, we must now include the jawanda."

"Proceeding on new course, Captain," Sulu announced, "warp-factor three."

Kirk had a sudden thought. "Mr. Spock, the Boquian mechanism restricts us to a maximum speed of warp-three. Ask Hivar how fast a jawanda can travel."

The reply took longer than usual. "No faster than our present velocity, Captain . . . or so it is believed. There is no way Hivar can say for certain, since its race was always concerned with putting distance between them and the jawanda and not closing it."

Kirk found himself once again trying to adjust to the idea of a creature which could move at a speed exceeding light. It made no sense—but then, the universe was full of things which did not make sense.

"Quarry is traveling at an angle to us, Captain. There is no indication that it has taken notice of our presence. We are proceeding on an intercept course which will bring us to capture range within twenty hours."

But it was a day longer before the extremely long-range visual sensors were able to pick anything up. There was a pause while Sulu adjusted instrumentation—and then they were gifted with their first sight of a jawanda.

It was all at once more magnificent and unexpected than Kirk had anticipated: an enormous rippling rectangular shape. The sensors were observing it from its flat side; otherwise, as with Saturn's rings, there would have been almost nothing to see. Were it not for the fluorescent colors which ran rippling across its featureless surface, even the computer-enhanced visual pickups would have shown nothing. The dancing lights, radiation consumed and transformed, gave outline and dimension to the creature.

"Looks like a big plastic sheet trying to digest an aurora," McCoy offered.

"Details, Mr. Spock?" Preliminary measurements?"

Spock was bent over readouts and indicators. "Its method of locomotion is unknown, Captain, though it appears to throw off energy as well as to absorb it. Thickness is apparently constant from one end to the other, with no significant tapering at either end."

"How thick, Mr. Spock?"

"Approximately one millimeter, Captain. Viewed from the side, even at close range, the creature would effectively vanish. By contrast, its length and breadth are considerable."

"You're starting to sound as vague as a Lactran, Spock," grumbled McCoy.

"It is difficult to estimate its surface area, Doctor."

"Why—because some of it appears edge-on?"

"No—because there is so much of it, and because the rectangular appearance is only approximate." He looked up from his readouts and gazed straight at Kirk. "I would say that this particular specimen is capable of covering most of the North American continent on Earth . . . though, of course, only to a depth of one millimeter, and that assuming the continent to be uniformly flat. Actual surface area is concomitantly somewhat less."

"That's . . . all right, Spock," Kirk assured his first officer, when he had his voice back. "It's big enough for our needs—and the Lactrans'." He sat staring at the unimaginably huge creature. Electric purples, mauve, metallic green, and azure drifted through its nearly transparent vastness, the discharges ample evidence of continual energy transfer.

"As a collector of stray radiation, it is a wonderfully designed organism," commented an admiring Spock.

"It maximizes surface-collection area while minimizing mass. Absorbed radiation is converted into operating substance and at least two kinds of radiant discharge. One is the radio wave we detect, while the other doubtless propels it through the cosmos in some fashion we do not yet fathom. I would give ten years of my life to know how it does this."

"If we can capture it, the Lactrans may give you the chance to find out, Spock."

"Captain!" Kirk looked sharply at Sulu. "It's changing course."

"Spock, ask Hivar if we're within capture distance yet."

Quickly now: "No, Captain. Hivar says we must move considerably closer before the mechanism can be effectively employed."

Sulu spoke again. "Definitely senses us, sir—moving almost directly away from us now."

"Speed, Lieutenant?"

"Warp-three, sir."

Kirk rubbed tiredly at his forehead. "Can it sense a trap?"

"Most certainly it can detect the gravitational fields of the six moons trailing us, Captain," Spock pointed out.

"If that's the case, then we're going to have trouble getting close to any of the beasts." He considered a moment and decided, "Let's continue following for another half day. It may grow tired."

But as he made his way back to his cabin to sleep, he found himself skeptical of outlasting a being which existed comfortably in the space between galaxies . . .

Sure enough, when he returned to the bridge he found the jawanda still traveling with apparent ease at warp-three, directly away from them. They had not closed the distance by a meter.

The simplicity of the dilemma didn't lessen Kirk's frustration. If they accelerated to warp-four, they would overtake the fleeing quarry—but without the means necessary to capture it. And there was something else he was beginning to wonder about, some-

thing which intruded on his thoughts to the point
where he found it necessary to put the question to their
guests, via Spock.

"Is a jawanda dangerous, Mr. Spock?"

"Hivar does not know, Captain, nor do the Lactrans.
The Boquian mechanism was always operated from
ground control, never from a ship. Hivar actually has
no idea how a jawanda might react to one—particularly one moving free of the protection of a strong
gravitational zone."

"I thought our guest considered it impolite to read
thoughts," Kirk observed mildly.

"Hivar apologizes, Captain, but replies that the
image in your mind was so strong it could not ignore
it."

The image the Boqus was referring to involved
Kirk's proposal to drop clear of the trailing moons and
proceed at a higher speed to overtake the jawanda.

"Once we do that," Kirk concluded, "we'll have to
find some way of turning the creature back toward the
six satellites."

"Hivar is not certain," Spock relayed slowly, "that
this is a good idea. Despite its apparent fragility, a
jawanda remains a being of unknown defensive capabilities, but one through which courses a good deal of
controlled energy. Hivar desires that its ignorance of
such abilities not serve as a pretext for foolhardy action."

"I see. What is the Lactrans' opinion?"

"They are of a similar mind, though equally uncertain."

"Does any of them have any better ideas?"

A hopeful wait, after which Spock declared, "They
do not, Captain. Free space is not the element of
Boqus or Lactrans. It belongs to the jawanda—and, at
present, to us far-ranging primitives. The Lactrans
concede that you must make the decision."

"What of Hivar?" Kirk pressed, knowing that without the Boqus's cooperation further pursuit of the
jawanda was useless.

"As Hivar can think of no alternative save to disengage and search for a jawanda at a more favorable intercept angle—"

"Which might not happen for that proverbial hundred years," Kirk pointed out sharply.

"—he consents, reluctantly, to follow your designated course of action."

"Tell him to break free of the six moons, then."

"He has already done so, Captain. He adds that—" but Kirk had no time now to listen to the cautions and concerns of Hivar the Toq, or the superior-minded Lactrans. Primitive creature or not, it had been given to him and his fellow savages to successfully bring to a conclusion this unique hunt.

For the first time since they'd left Lactra, he felt in complete command of his ship.

"Mr. Sulu!" he barked. "Mr. Arex! Compute new course to bring us around and in behind the jawanda." Both helmsman and navigator rushed to comply.

Sulu looked back alertly moments later. "Course computed and laid in, sir."

"All ahead on new heading, warp-factor five," Kirk ordered.

Moving far faster than their quarry now, the *Enterprise* leaped ahead, circling in a great arc around the fleeting creature, the ship's powerful engine enabling it to all but vanish from the jawanda's immediate vicinity.

"Any indication it's detected us, Mr. Spock?" he finally asked when they were moving toward the creature instead of away from it. The *Enterprise*'s science officer studied the information fed back by long-range scanners.

"Apparently it has not changed direction, Captain. Either it is convinced we are still in pursuit, or it believes itself no longer threatened."

Distance shortened rapidly. "Reduce speed to warp-two, Mr. Sulu. Let's see if dropping to a velocity below its capabilities affects it."

"Still no change, Captain," reported Spock seconds later. "Coming directly toward us." A pause; then: "Hivar the Toq expresses some concern."

"Thank Hivar for its concern," replied Kirk, too

busy now to worry about diplomatic niceties. "Slow to warp-factor one, Mr. Sulu."

"Slowing, Captain. I have visual contact." A quick adjustment and the jawanda appeared again on the viewscreen forward. Only now the sparkling, rippling shape, a living microthin continent, was charging toward them at warp-three.

"It's beginning to slow, Captain," Sulu reported, a touch of anxiety in his voice. "Still coming toward us, though."

"Phasers on low power, Lieutenant."

"Phasers, sir?" the helmsman inquired uncertainly.

"That's right. We're going to try to turn it back toward the six moons of the Boquian mechanism. Fire as soon as it comes within range." If it comes within range, he added silently.

"Creature is slowing . . . warp-two . . . warp-one . . . range still decreasing . . . it's not going to turn or stop in time, sir."

"Fire, Mr. Sulu." Kirk leaned forward and gripped the arms of the command chair tightly. If they killed it, they'd have to begin another search.

"Firing," came the helmsman's even reply. Two dull blue beams jumped across the shrinking gap toward the onrushing monster, struck the ever-twisting surface . . . to no apparent effect.

"No indication of reaction from the jawanda, Captain," Spock informed him.

"Still coming at us, sir." Sulu looked back at the command chair for instructions.

"Increase phaser power to half strength, Mr. Sulu. Fire."

Once more the two beams, this time shining far more brightly in the darkness, crossed the space between ship and jawanda. It reacted this time, slowing even further—but for some reason Kirk felt that the decrease in velocity had nothing to do with the *Enterprise*'s attack.

It continued to rush toward them.

"Full power, Mr. Sulu!" he ordered hastily. All that could be seen ahead now was the lightninglike display of color rippling through the jawanda's substance as it transformed and dissipated untold energy with the ease of an earthworm digesting dirt.

This time the two beams which touched the creature were intense enough to blind, had not the ship's battle computer automatically compensated for the anticipated brilliance by suitably adjusting the forward scanners.

Those two beams, striking with the full energy of the *Enterprise* behind them, were capable of piercing the thick hull of any vessel in existence, of reducing mountains to rubble and boiling away small seas. They struck the underside (or perhaps the topside) of the jawanda.

Flexible, incredibly tough cells contracted, reacted where the beams hit. That enormous surface curled like foil in five-hundred-kilometer-wide swirls.

But it did not stop, did not turn aside, and did not slow further.

"We're going to crash, Jim," McCoy murmured fatalistically, his fascinated gaze frozen on the viewscreen.

"All decks, red alert, Lieutenant Uhura. Brace for collision! Mr. Sulu, evasion course, warp-six—emergency gravity compensation!"

Engines operating near idle suddenly gulped great amounts of energy as abrupt demands were made on the ship's warp-drive units. The *Enterprise* shot forward and to one side—three-quarters of a second too late.

A thin filament of jawanda, a living peninsula, caught the ship's secondary hull. It was a small extension of the creature—probably only a few hundred kilometers long and wide.

A gentle shudder went through the fabric of the ship. It was felt on the bridge, in the recreation rooms, in Engineering, throughout. One by one the exterior scanners went dim as they were covered by jawanda.

The body of the monster was so thin that at first the scanners could penetrate its substance. This lasted until the jawanda began to fold in on itself, burying the hull in more and more of its body, millimeter piling on millimeter, until the cruiser was completely enveloped in successive folds of jawanda.

"Slow again to warp-factor two, Mr. Sulu." The helmsman complied, but the action had no effect on the jawanda. It continued to turn in on itself, still only millimeters thick, but growing deeper and thicker, like sediment deposited by some strange intergalactic stream. Total darkness soon showed on the screen as the jawanda's density finally grew impenetrable.

"I've seen a spider do the same thing to its prey," McCoy muttered, "wrapping it again and again in folds of silk. When it's finished, it bites through the silk and—"

"Don't arachnemorphize, Doctor," interrupted Spock.

McCoy blinked, his morbid visualizations temporarily shattered. "Don't *what?*"

"Don't ascribe spiderlike characteristics to an alien being."

"Captain?"

Kirk bent quickly to the intercom. "What is it, Scotty?"

"I dinna know for sure, sir. We're puttin' out as much power as usual, but for some reason it's not being utilized properly in the engines."

"Mr. Sulu," Kirk asked tightly, "what's our speed?"

"Warp-two, Captain . . . no, wait a minute." The helmsman studied his instruments in disbelief. "That is, we're supposed to be moving at warp-two—but we're not. In fact, we seem to be slowing!"

"I believe I know what is happening, Captain." Kirk looked over at Spock, could sense Vulcan mind-wheels turning rapidly. "The jawanda is an energy converter, and a remarkably efficient one. We are currently putting out a tremendous amount of radiant energy, compared to what it normally receives in the comparative emptiness of intergalactic space. This energy is highly concentrated, yet available without the threat of an attendant gravitational field. To the jawanda the *Enterprise* must seem a magical apparition of the greatest delicacy.

"Naturally, it wishes to maximize this unexpected new food source. By enveloping us in repeated folds of its absorbtive surface, it is logically attempting to contain all the radiant energy we produce, trying to prevent it from escaping into free space."

"Warp-factor one, Captain," came an excited voice from the speaker at Kirk's elbow. "Dilithium crystals showing stress patterns along interval cleavage planes," the chief engineer added. "If we don't shut down the drive now, sir, we risk losin' any chance of reactivatin' it."

Suddenly the awesome depths of the intergalactic gulf were pressing intimately around Kirk's mind. The very possibility of becoming trapped out here, many light-years away from the outermost fringes of the Milky Way, let alone the Federation, was not pleasant to dwell upon.

"All right, Scotty, if you think it's that vital, shut down the converters. We'll use impulse power to maintain life-support functions only—and hope the jawanda isn't so starved it begins to drain that too."

"Aye, Captain."

Kirk heard him shouting commands to assistants and subordinates. His concern paramount, Scotty even forgot to sign off.

Kirk closed the open link to Engineering himself. A low whine rose in intensity for a brief moment, then faded to silence, the dying wheeze of an electronic zephyr. For an instant the lights on the bridge flickered confusedly before the changeover was complete. They brightened again, as strong as before, dimmer only in Kirk's anxious imagination.

"Any comments on our situation from our alien guests, Mr. Spock?" the captain inquired hopefully.

Spock listened and informed him, "Hivar the Toq had not considered the possibility that the ship's radiation might prove an attraction to the jawanda. Conversely, the Lactrans are delighted."

"Nice to know that the present predicament is pleasing to someone," McCoy murmured sardonically.

"They commend you on your speed in capturing one

so easily and in such a subtle fashion, and wonder how soon we can begin the return journey to Lactra."

"That's fine, Spock, except our friends have things a bit mixed up. It's the jawanda who's captured us, not the other way around." Kirk thought several uncomplimentary things about Lactrans, for the moment not caring particularly if his emanations were detected. Still, he mused, their present troubles were not the fault of the Lactrans. Nor of Hivar the Toq, whose knowledge of jawandas had admittedly extended no further than the atmosphere of Boqu.

"It is possible, Captain," Spock added, "that the creature will depart the *Enterprise* of its own accord, now that the main generator of radiation on board has been shut down. I do not think we should wait for this dubious eventuality. Somehow we must make it release the ship, at least long enough to permit us to get safely underway, at a speed sufficient to prevent a recurrence of the present awkward situation."

Awkward! McCoy shouted silently, amazed as ever at the first officer's capacity for understatement.

"It certainly can't worsen our difficulties to make the attempt, Spock," agreed a thoughtful Kirk. He studied the blanked-out scanners for a moment, then decided, "Let's take a firsthand look at what we're dealing with. Bones, you come too."

McCoy glanced at him curiously. " 'Come'? Come where, Jim?"

"Outside, of course. We can't tell very much about the jawanda from in here."

While McCoy gaped at Kirk, Spock wondered easily, "Shall I contact Chief Kyle, Captain?"

Kirk made a negative gesture. "No, Mr. Spock—no transporters. The creature could drain the power from the transporter as fast as it was renewed, though I don't think it would notice such a small output of channeled radiation. But I am concerned that the transporter beam might fail to penetrate the energy-sensitive substance of the creature's body. Remember what Hivar told us about its screening capabilities? Rather than take that indeterminate risk, we'll go out

STAR TREK LOG EIGHT 139

through one of the emergency-access ports—and hope the jawanda doesn't decide to suck the energy from our life-support belts."

Before long the three men found themselves standing within the lock of the emergency port nearest the bridge, on the upper section of the ship's primary hull.

"Activate life-support systems," Kirk ordered. Lime-yellow auras instantly enveloped them all. Kirk saw by McCoy's approving nod that his own system was functioning properly. That slim yellowish halo was all that stood between them and the absolute cold of intergalactic space.

"Cycle the lock, Mr. Spock." The first officer touched the necesary switch, and the exterior door began to slide aside. Kirk felt a slight pull as the wisps of atmosphere missed by the ship's recyclers rushed out through the widening gap.

Looking out, he saw only the expected darkness. Yet there *was* something different about it. There should not have been a total absence of distant light, but there was.

Putting out an aura-shielded hand, he encountered resistence where none was expected. A slick rubbery wall sealed the lock exit, though the slickness was more imagined than felt, since his fingers did not actually make contact with the jawanda's body. Experimentally, he pushed. The dark material gave with surprising flexibility. Kirk had had no idea what to expect—something hard and resistant, perhaps, or soft like dark jelly. Instead, there was only this easily elastic smoothness.

For a moment he wondered if this was actually the body of their continent-sized nemesis. Then he jumped slightly as several small purple coruscations ran in uneven spurts across the living surface before them. The jawanda was sweating fire.

"Wonderful creature," Spock murmured.

"Let's admire it from a distance, Spock," suggested McCoy tersely. "What about trying a phaser on it, Jim?"

"Mr. Spock?" Kirk stepped back from the exit and

regarded the dark substance expectantly as Spock removed the small hand phaser from his waist. The first officer set the beam on low power and directed it outward.

Blue light touched the black film blocking the doorway. Where it contacted the surface of the creature the material began to glow. The dark substance turned a light yellow at first. This melted rapidly into orange, then red, and finally into a rich purple. The mild assault was exquisitely beautiful and wholy ineffective.

"Try more power, Spock," Kirk advised. Spock did so, gradually adjusting the phaser until it was on maximum. The intense emissions produced only a slight rippling in the jawanda's body, causing it to retreat outward about half a meter from the edge of the lock.

Of course, this could have been due to sheer enjoyment of the radiation bath as much as to discomfort or injury.

"That's enough, Mr. Spock," Kirk finally declared. The first officer flipped off the phaser and reset it on his waist. Kirk was only slightly disappointed. He hadn't really expected that the tiny phaser would be capable of threatening the enormous organism.

"It absorbs energy like a sponge, Captain," commented Spock.

"What about the ship's main phasers this close to it?" wondered McCoy.

Spock considered, "I think the effect would be essentially the same as before, Doctor: a futile waste of energy. There is so much jawanda to dissipate so little power ... and it could put a severe strain on our already dangerously weakened power supply."

Kirk studied the blank wall of living material. The purple glow was fading slowly, contentedly. "What about the possibilities of a biological assault, Bones? Some sort of injection?"

McCoy almost laughed. "On a creature the size of North America? As thin as it is, I think it would handle the most massive dose I could give it the same way Spock says it would a blast from our main phasers—by dissipating it throughout its body. That's assuming I could concoct something able to affect its body. There doesn't appear to be anything remotely resembling a central nerve center, or even nerves. They might exist, but even if the creature allowed it, we could vivisect a few dozen kilometers and miss any vital points by a week's march.

"No, thanks, I'm not ready to tackle this. Give me a nice simple problem instead, like solving a Boquian epidemic." He gestured helplessly at the black film blockading the exit. "I'm sorry, Jim, but there's nothing I can do."

"Then that leaves one thing," Kirk said determinedly, "that we haven't tried." After double-checking to insure that the gravity specifics of his life-support system were engaged, he walked forward, put both hands against the dark skin—and shoved hard.

The jawanda's body parted like a torn sheet, and Kirk's hands went right through.

Rather than expressing satisfaction, he sounded abashed. "We overlooked the obvious in favor of the technical. A common mistake of mechanically minded civilizations." Using his hands, he widened the gap. The substance resisted steadily, but continued to give way under the captain's firm pressure.

"Follow me." Stepping carefully through the hole, he walked out onto the surface of the jawanda.

They emerged facing rearward. Instead of the sloping back of the *Enterprise*'s primary hull, flanked by the two torpedo shapes of the warp-drive propulsion units, they saw only a black formlessness. It turned the streamlined cruiser into a dark nebula of constantly shifting outline.

A long tail like the back of a black comet stretched into the distance aft, glowing now and then with vibrant sparks and the random chromatic streaks of internal lightning.

"Wonder what we look like from a distance," McCoy murmured aloud, at once amazed and appalled by the sight.

"The cape of some fantastic giant," Kirk hypothesized, "or the image of legended Azathoth ... We've become a child's dream, Bones."

"Or its nightmare," McCoy countered.

"It is conceivable," Spock ventured, refusing to be drawn into such useless, illogical speculation, "that by utilizing the manual labor of the entire ship's complement we could physically remove the creature from the hull. However, this would prove futile in the end, since there is no way to prevent it from reestablishing itself once all hands have returned inside."

"I dislike the thought of totally abandoning the ship to automatics, even for a few minutes," Kirk added as they made their way across the black substance. It rippled eerily underfoot wherever an aura-clad boot touched down, like concentric circles fleeing a stone flung into a pond.

Kirk put a foot down with experimental firmness, then raised it quickly. Gently the material reformed itself over the exposed circlet of metal, apparently undamaged. Leaning over, he peered intently at the dark flesh, but could detect nothing resembling a seam or repaired wound.

"Remarkably efficient in all ways," Spock declared, also studying the area where Kirk's foot had pressed down.

"Yes. It seems to—" He broke off, staring rearward.

"What is it, Jim?" a worried McCoy inquired.

"Is it my imagination, Bones, or is the jawanda starting to move?"

McCoy looked around, and even as he watched the activity Kirk thought he had sensed increased visibly. "No, I see it too, Jim."

At the edges the colossal mass seemed to be rippling and fluttering with greater violence. A moment later their life-support belts reacted to similar action underfoot, keeping the men firmly attached to the immediate surface beneath them as it too began to move up and down in increasingly higher arcs.

"Captain, I think it best that we reenter the ship, at least until this sudden activity subsides."

"You won't get any argument from me, Spock," admitted Kirk readily. He was already moving as fast as possible back toward the open hatchway. Despite the knowledge that the life-support systems would hold them tight to the jawanda, he had to fight down an urge to drop flat and hug the surface.

"Why do you think it's reacting like this, Spock?"

"There may be any number of reasons, Captain," the first officer responded, a smooth thrust of body-substance sending him arching meters above Kirk and McCoy. Then Spock had dropped into a low pit and they were looking down at him.

"Possibly it is irritated by our presence, though I think that unlikely. It may be seeking to realign itself to further maximize its energy gathering potential. Or ..." He paused. "It is possible that, with the ship's warp-drive units deactivated, the reason for its enveloping the *Enterprise*—to be wrapped tightly about a source of intense and now vanished radiation—has disappeared. It may be preparing to leave."

"Then I suggest we hurry," advised McCoy, exercising a bit of understatment himself as he increased his pace.

After another couple of minutes had passed, Kirk slowed his progress across the rolling surface. Frowning, he muttered, "We should have reached the hatchway by now." Turning in a slow circle, he examined the living terrain behind them. All was shifting, hilly blackness. No comforting light showed through.

"As a matter of fact, how are we going to relocate it? The jawanda is so dense now that the light from the lock can't penetrate it."

There was silence, each man wrapped in his own thoughts. Then McCoy said hesitantly, pointing, "I think it was over that way, Jim."

Slowly they retraced what they hoped had been their original steps—slowly so that they wouldn't overrun the lock entrance, and also because the jawanda was now heaving up and down in twenty-meter-high ripples. Only plenty of experience working in low-g environments kept them from becoming violently ill.

After five minutes McCoy had to admit that his

guess had been wrong. Kirk and Spock were equally disoriented.

"It is imperative that we do not continue to search blindly about, Captain," Spock declared, his even, controlled tones a great comfort in the fleshy chaos heaving around them. "I believe we must risk the utilization of transporter energy to have ourselves beamed back into the ship. So long as the jawanda remains attached to the hull, we will never locate the open lock."

"I agree," McCoy added quickly, the distant glow of the Milky Way galaxy bobbing drunkenly behind them. "Even though the creature hasn't threatened us, I don't like the idea of being stuck out here as our life-support charges run down."

"We don't know for certain that the jawanda is harmless, Doctor," Spock observed coolly, not enhancing McCoy's current state of mind.

Kirk nodded his assent to Spock, who removed his communicator from his waist and flipped it open. His words carried to his two companions as he addressed the open speaker grid.

"Spock to Main Transporter Room, Spock to Main Transporter Room." There was a silent pause. The first officer looked across at Kirk. "Acknowledge, Transporter Room." Still no reply. "Nothing, Captain—not even normal background noise."

"Maybe your communicator is malfunctioning, Spock," Kirk suggested. Reaching down, he opened his own instrument. "This is the captain speaking. Transporter Room . . . bridge . . . anyone receiving, please acknowledge." Only the emptiness of space sounded from the tiny grid.

"I should have guessed," Spock broke in, in his own quiet way furious with himself. "Naturally the energy-screening abilities of the jawanda blocks out the weak waves produced by our communicators. There is only—"

Despite superhuman balance, he lurched forward as the surface moved beneath them. Kirk nearly fell backward, and McCoy tumbled flat.

The jawanda, its primary source of radiation now

completely cut off, was once again feeling the need to spread its energy-gathering bulk as wide as possible to gather the stray radiation drifting across the intergalactic gulf. The violent contraction which had thrown everyone off balance was caused by the creature's beginning to separate from the *Enterprise*.

Kirk fought to keep from screaming in panic as the starfield wheeled crazily around them. The energy-eater finally straightened out, having unwound itself from the hull.

Looking back, Kirk saw the *Enterprise* behind them. It was shrinking at a terrifying pace at the tail end of a vast dark carpet.

Ahead of them lay nothing but black infinity . . .

X

Kirk rolled over and managed to sit up. "Communicators, Spock. There's nothing to screen them out now." But his first officer was already reaching for the compact instrument, flipping the top open.

"Spock to *Enterprise,* Spock to *Enterprise* . . . Come in, *Enterprise.*"

A faint voice barely recognizable as that of the ship's helmsman issued from the speaker, weak with increasing distance and distorted by the crackle of radiant discharge from the jawanda beneath them.

"Mr. Spock . . . what's happened? Our scanners are operating again. The jawanda has broken free and—"

"Transport us back aboard, Mr. Sulu," Spock interrupted urgently. "Immediately."

"What's that, Mr. Spock? I can't . . ." There was a burst of static. ". . . quite hear you." Dimly they heard, "Sensors seem to indicate you are no longer on the ship's hull. What—"

"Activate engines!" Spock ordered crisply. "Follow

the jawanda and overtake. We are stranded on the jawanda, repeat, *on the jawanda*. It is moving out of visual range. We are—"

"Never mind, Spock," McCoy advised, an odd tinge in his voice, "they can't hear us any more."

But Spock persisted, his voice never breaking as he continued broadcasting. Rapidly the *Enterprise* became a shapeless dot, then a star ... and soon was lost to sight as the jawanda sped away at a rate no living creature should have been able to attain.

Three men more isolated than any in the universe sat themselves with unnatural calm on the thin surface of their unbelievable steed and took stock of their situation.

It was not promising.

"We are fairly sure the *Enterprise* is faster than the jawanda," Spock noted, "but it must get underway rapidly in order to be able to track us." Glancing to the side, he saw the vast circle of the home galaxy dominating the darkness like a gigantic pinwheel.

"Even if they temporarily lose contact with us," McCoy pointed out, with more confidence than he felt, "they ought to be able to pick up the energy field surrounding the creature. We located it in empty space once before, by the sound it emits. No reason why Sulu and Uhura shouldn't be able to do it again." He essayed a timorous smile.

"All very true, Doctor," an almost but not quite shaky Vulcan voice agreed, "unless the ship's instrumentation locks onto *another* of the creatures. If that happens and the ship follows a different jawanda for even a short while, we could be carried far beyond easy sensor range."

"Thanks, Spock," McCoy muttered morosely. "I can always depend on you to cheer me up." Absently he ran a hand over the smooth obsidian film beneath them. Glowing phosphorescence trailed his hand, like the night wake produced by a boat traveling one of Earth's oceans. "I've been marooned on several worlds and a few moons before, but never on a living creature."

"We've discovered a flying carpet that would astound humanity's ancient story-tellers," Kirk mused. "I wonder where it's carrying us."

It was amazing, he reflected, how rapidly he had adjusted to the possibility they might never be found. At least they would die in space, and quickly, when the energy powering their life-support belts gave out or was drained away by the jawanda. His gaze moved again to the lambent spiral of the Milky Way. A more fitting subject for the final sight of a starship captain could not be imagined . . .

As had so often been the case in times past, Captain Kirk's resignation proved premature. Spock had been standing rigid for long moments, almost at attention. When he spoke again, his voice was relaxed.

"There is no need for concern any longer, Captain. The *Enterprise* is tracking us."

McCoy scrambled to his feet, and together he and Kirk stared rearward—or at least in the direction Spock was facing; it was impossible to determine true direction. Kirk strained, could see nothing but distant star clusters and nebulae, not even a moving point which might turn out to be the ship.

"How can you tell, Spock? I can't make out a thing."

"I am in communication with one on board. The connection at this distance is tenuous, but with no other intelligent minds around us—"

"The Lactrans!" McCoy exclaimed.

"Yes, the Lactrans," Spock confirmed. "While they have been unable to assist in the capture of the jawanda, it seems that their presence has produced an unexpected but welcome benefit. The young one is in communication with its parents, who relay instructions through it to Mr. Sulu and Mr. Arex."

Shortly thereafter the most beautiful sight in the universe hove into view: the *Enterprise*. It grew to the size of a small flower and finally loomed huge behind them.

Or perhaps now it was before them, since they seemed to be rushing toward it. Kirk studied the ship as the first fold of jawanda reached outward. Spock's comment mirrored his own thoughts.

"The creature is once more rushing at the *Enterprise,* sensing the nearness of renewed radiation from her engines."

Behind them, a towering black wave was curling overhead, arcing downward like an onyx tsunami. It blotted out the bright glow of the home galaxy, surged ahead and downward. All three men had to fight down an unusual tendency to claustrophobia as the black curtain descended on them. No crushing weight shoved them flat as they hurried toward the nearing hull. The blackness settled with feathery lightness. Each time a new fold of jawanda curled over them, they pushed upward with stiff arms and forced a temporary gap in the creature's body, emerging into the starlight again and again.

Finally the jawanda stopped wrapping itself about the ship. They found themselves standing once more on a black-coated hull, unable to recognize a single feature through the amorphous structure of the creature.

"We're right back where we started," McCoy observed, sighing heavily. "I can't say I'm disappointed."

"On the contrary, Doctor, we are not back where we started," objected Spock. "I am still in contact with the Lactrans." Turning slowly, he faced toward the front of the ship and pointed. "That way."

Following the first officer's lead, they walked over to an area which looked no different from any other, or from the one they'd just left. Spock gestured slightly ahead and down. "We're here, Captain."

Kneeling uncertainly, Kirk reached out and shoved with both hands. Once again the multiple folds of jawanda parted—but this time a gleam appeared in the opening thus produced. It was the most welcome sight Kirk had seen in a long time.

Widening the gap with his hands and with McCoy's help, they were soon able to slip back into the comforting closeness of the emergency lock. Undamaged, the jawanda reformed behind them, shutting out the universe once more.

Spock activated the lock and it cycled shut behind them. Atmosphere was automatically pumped into the chamber as soon as the airtight telltale went on, and the all-clear sounded a second later. Gratefully, Kirk deactivated his life-support belt, as did Spock and McCoy. The doctor opened the inner door.

A large, cylindrical mass the color of lead filled the corridor beyond. Kirk still could not tell when the young Lactran was standing or sitting—or if those terms had any referent to Lactrans. He had the impression that the youthful alien was regarding them attentively.

"It apologizes, Captain," Spock announced.

"Apologizes?" Kirk wondered if the surprise was as clear in his mind as it was in his voice. "Its parents just saved our lives." He returned the creature's eyeless stare. "We are more grateful than we can—"

"Nevertheless, it persists in its apologetic attitude, Captain. The sudden disengagement of the jawanda which carried us away from the ship caught it and its parents by surprise."

"They weren't the only ones," Kirk countered feelingly.

"They are sorry for the delay incurred in directing the ship to us, and hope that our simple minds have not suffered any damage as a result of this negligence."

"Tell them our primitive cognitive apparatus is functioning normally," Kirk replied with a grin. "If they hadn't acted when they did, we wouldn't be functioning at all."

Making a strange weaving motion with its multiple-digited front end, the Lactran adolescent turned and scuttled off down the corridor.

"It begs to be excused, Captain. It wishes to visit its parents. The strain involved in reaching across such a distance has weakened them. We must return to the hunt, they insist—with the foreknowledge that this time they may not be able to help us."

"From now on we're going to stay inside the ship,"

declared McCoy. "You can tell them that, Spock." He
turned to Kirk. "What now, Jim?" he asked as he set
his life-support belt in its proper rack, making sure the
recharge light was on.

"Back to the Bridge, Bones. From there ... I don't
know. Any ideas?"

Neither McCoy nor Spock had come up with the
hoped-for miracle solution by the time the turbolift deposited them on the bridge. Kirk acknowledged the
warm yet restrained welcomes of the crew as Spock
moved to his science station. McCoy relaxed nearby.

"I have a small theory, Captain," Spock announced,
sitting down in his chair.

"Pursue it, Mr. Spock." The first officer's theories
often turned out to be more solidly grounded than
many supposed facts. Spock bent to the library-computer console with a will.

Glancing at the main viewscreen, Kirk was rewarded
with the expected picture of dull blackness occasionally
enlivened by scratchy streaks of maroon-and-emerald
lightning.

"Status, Mr. Sulu?"

This time it was not necessary for the helmsman to
check his instrumentation. "The jawanda has once
more enveloped the *Enterprise,* Captain. As soon as we
learned that you were safely back aboard, Mr. Scott
deactivated the drive again." Sulu gazed uncertainly
back at him. "What do we try now, sir?"

"I don't know, Lieutenant." Kirk considered. "For
our purposes the creature reacts favorably to physical
pressure, but I can't have hundreds of people out on
the hull shoving and pushing. Energy weapons are useless against it—in fact, they probably strengthen it. A
photon torpedo might have some effect, but we can't
very well explode one against the creature when its
body is only millimeters from the ship. Besides, we
want to capture it whole, not chop it to pieces. The
devil of it is, we have the jawanda right where we want
it. Only we can't use the warp-drive engines to carry it
and ourselves back to Lactra."

"A moment, Captain," Spock requested, as Kirk was

trying to think of a way to utilize the jawanda's docility under physical pressure. The first officer was bent over the main readout from the library-computer console.

"I am concluding certain calculations. There." He looked up, staring for a moment into nothingness, before turning to Kirk and informing him, "The Lactrans also believe the idea is feasible, though dangerous. They refuse to support or to reject the proposal."

"What proposal?" Kirk wondered guardedly.

"To impel the jawanda to release us by providing too much of what it wants. In a word, we shall appeal to its sense of gluttony."

"I'm not sure I understand what you're driving at, Spock."

"Consider, Captain. When we collided with the creature we were moving, according to final readout, at warp-four, coming up to warp-six, which we never fully attained. If we suddenly fed a sustained burst of emergency power to the engines, the equivalent of warp-factor seven or eight, it is possible that the surfeit of energy—of food—would dangerously strain the creature's absorptive capacities.

"It would have two choices: to burst from overconsumption or abandon its hold on the *Enterprise*. If the former happens, we will at least be free to search for another jawanda, with our knowledge of its abilities and habits enlarged. If the latter, we may be able to engage the Boquian mechanism before the engorged creature can escape."

"It sounds good," admitted McCoy hopefully. "Why are the Lactrans leery of trying it?"

"Their reasons are twofold, Doctor. Should the jawanda *not* be overloaded by the surge of energy, we run the risk as stated by Engineer Scott of losing our warp-drive capability altogether. This would leave us with only impulse power on which to recross a considerable amount of space." His gaze momentarily checked a figure displayed on one of the science station's several screens.

"On impulse power it would take us approximately three hundred and sixty-five standard years to reach the outskirts of our galaxy, with the Federation a good deal farther away. That is assuming the engine components last that long."

"Let's hope we don't have to try it," Kirk said. "What about our guests' other concern?"

"It has already been mentioned, Captain," Spock declared. "They worry about damage to the specimen."

Kirk forebore formulating his first thoughts. It wouldn't do to insult someone who had just saved your life.

"Any other proposals, Spock?" he asked, hoping for an alternative that carried less of an air of finality.

"I am afraid not, Captain. This course of action seems to offer our best hope of breaking clear."

Kirk sighed and activated the armchair pickup. "Engineering?"

"Scott here. What is it, Captain?"

"Scotty, this creature drinks radiant energy. Since we can't pull away from it, we're going to have to try to convince it to let us go—by generating a cosmic bellyache. Somehow we've got to overfeed it. I'm going to want maximum emergency power from the converters for as long as you can provide it."

"Aye, Captain," the chief engineer assented reluctantly. "I dinna know how long we can maintain it, the way that monster drains our production."

"We want it to drain us, Scotty—until it's sick of it. Keep the converters functioning for as long as you can. This *has* to work."

"I understand, Captain," Scott replied solemnly. "Engineerin' out."

Kirk clicked off and looked forward. "Mr. Arex?" The Edoan navigator acknowledged, his bony-ridged skull turning three soulful eyes on the captain.

"Yes, sir?"

"If we do succeed in breaking free of the creature, we're going to want to come back for it . . . monumental pain in the stern that it's been. We're liable to break completely free at warp-seven or warp-eight, so you'll have to try to retain a position fix on it."

"I'll manage, Captain."

"I know you will, Mr. Arex." He studied first the living dark matter covering the scanner, then the viewscreen, while searching for a flaw in Spock's reasoning and finding none. How many times, he mused, had he found himself betting his existence and that of his crew on a cut of the deck by Fate. *His* record for turning up aces was unblemished . . . so far. It was time again to try to extend the streak: "Mr. Sulu, all ahead warp-factor seven, emergency power."

"Engaged, Captain," came the response from the helm.

A steady whine began to sound, more felt than audible. It rose to a pitch just shy of setting everyone's teeth on edge, then held steady. Instead of the normal rush of lights across the screen, they continued to see only blackness. A minute passed, two, three . . . Angry jagged bolts of crimson and gold began to race bizarrely through that living film. Four minutes, five . . .

"It doesn't seem to be having any effect, Captain," Spock reported calmly, his gaze locked to the gooseneck viewer. "The jawanda is still wrapped completely around us."

"Increase to maximum emergency overdrive, Mr. Sulu." Kirk said. "Warp-factor eight."

Sulu hesitated the briefest instant, started to look backward, then murmured a tight "Yes, sir" instead.

The whine became a painful drone like the keening of a single gigantic bee. Kirk felt a faint throb through the metal structure of the command chair as the ship's fabric sought to remain intact under the enormous energies generated by her engines.

Six minutes, seven, eight . . . a voice shouting from the intercom, barely recognizable. "Captain, we canna hold this much longer! Converters are beginnin' to fail."

"Warp-factor seven, sir," Sulu suddenly announced. "Warp-factor six, five . . ."

Kirk snapped at the intercom. "Scotty, maintain full emergency power! Never mind protecting the converters now, we need everything you can—"

"That's what we're givin', Captain," the chief engineer countered. "I'm tryin' to tell you—the energy's not bein' translated into thrust. That thing's sucking up everything we can generate and searching for more."

"Warp-factor four," Sulu declared worriedly. The bone-grating whine of emergency overdrive had long since faded, along with its comforting throb of power.

"We must make a final decision immediately, Captain," exclaimed an anxious Spock, "or the converters will permanently collapse."

Kirk's gaze was fixed on the viewscreen, fascinated by the now continual display of lightning so brilliant the battle compensators were hard pressed to sop the intensity to below pain threshold. Every hue of the rainbow was present in those unending discharges as the jawanda fought to dissipate surplus energy. Kirk wished he could be floating free in space nearby. The trailing cometlike portion of the jawanda must present a spectacular sight. Indeed, an unsuspecting observer who chanced to pass through the immediate spatial vicinity would see jawanda and *Enterprise* as a colossal oblate opal, lit with internal fire.

Kirk was about to order an end to the seemingly futile effort when the colors vanished, revealing the far plainer but much more welcome isolated lights of distant galaxies pinwheeling through the gulf.

"We're clear!" McCoy yelped joyously.

"Disengagement confirmed, Doctor," concurred Spock, considerably less exuberantly. "It worked ... barely."

"The creature is falling rapidly off screen astern, sir," Arex announced, in a tone almost as relaxed as Spock's.

"Warp-factor five," Sulu declared, "factor six and increasing."

"Reduce speed to warp-four, Mr. Sulu!" Kirk ordered quickly. "Don't lose our quarry, Mr. Arex."

"Not to worry, Captain," the navigator assured him, examining his own sensor readouts. "It is now by far the most obvious object in the heavens, due to the amount of energy it continues to radiate."

"Plot a return curve to bring us directly back at the

creature, Mr. Arex. We can't waste time and allow it to
regain its flexibility in converting energy." He voiced a
quick question to the arm pickup: "Scotty—how are
the engines?"

"Recoverin' rapidly, Captain," the chief engineer reported, the strain of the last minutes evident in his
voice, "but it was a near thing. I wouldn't like to
chance it again."

"We're going to do our best not to, Scotty," the
Captain assured him, before clicking off. His stare
moved repeatedly from helm to viewscreen. "What
about the jawanda, Mr. Arex? Is it trying to escape?"

"It does not appear to be succeeding, if such is its
intention, sir," the Edoan announced carefully. "It is
moving away from us, but very slowly, and in an erratic manner."

"Bloated," McCoy decided firmly. "The overload
was too much for its converters to handle. I'd venture
to say that its whole system has been affected."

"The Lactrans," Spock put in, gazing momentarily
at the wall before him, "hope there is no permanent
damage."

"We do too," admitted Kirk, "so long as the alternative doesn't turn out to be rapid recovery."

"It is continuing to move away, Captain," Arex said
softly, "but more slowly now."

"Sensors indicate it is discharging energy at an incredible rate, Captain," declared Spock. "It may be regaining some of its ability."

"I wonder—Spock, do you think it's capable of anger?"

"I don't know, Captain. But the instinct to defend
oneself is basic to many very primitive organisms." He
eyed Kirk expectantly. "You have something in mind?"

"Somehow, Spock, we have to distract it long
enough for Hivar to engage the capture mechanism. If
the creature doesn't actually conceive of us as a threat,
it should at least regard the ship as a challenge. By
now it should be dazed and disoriented—its present
movements indicate that. I can only see one way to

draw it within range of the Boquian device—and that's
to tempt it into chasing us."

"Jim!" McCoy exclaimed, startled. "If it manages to
envelop us again . . ."

"I know it's a risk, Bones, but we've got full motive
power back. We'll have to cut it close, but if it gets too
close we can outspurt it at the last moment." I hope,
he added silently.

Spock helped him make up his mind. "I agree it
should be tried, Captain."

"What do the Lactrans think?"

Spock listened silently. "They are agreeable to anything which has as its final purpose the capture of a
jawanda."

"Good. Mr. Sulu, slow our speed gradually. I want it
to look like we're having trouble of our own."

"Slowing, Captain," the helmsman responded.
"Should I notify Engineering?"

Kirk considered and half smiled as he replied, "Better not, Lieutenant. I can guess Chief Scott's pic-
turesque opinion of this idea." He became all serious-
ness again as a pulsing spot appeared on the
viewscreen, an object the size of his thumbnail, a
seething pool of color.

Fat and sassy, he thought. Probably thickened its
waistline by an enormous amount—maybe even another whole millimeter. If the monster had the instincts
of an amoeba, it should be spoiling to defend itself
against anything that smacked of an attack—particularly an attack by a source of food. Still, the jawanda's
ability to relieve itself of excess energy remained an
unknown, unmeasurable factor. As important as the
time factor was, they would have to proceed with caution.

"Speed of target, Mr. Arex?"

"Still moving away from us, Captain, approximately
warp-factor one point two two."

"Spock, we're counting on its reacting like any other
living organism, but we still have no idea how advanced it really is. Any chance it could be intelligent?"

That, he thought, might complicate events considerably.

"I doubt it, Captain," the first officer declared, glancing up from his instrumentation. "Its instincts should be quite primitive. It gives every indication of existing only to perform three basal functions: eating, excreting, and reproducing."

"I agree. It better ... I'm tired of surprises, especially potentially lethal ones. Is Hivar the Toq ready?"

Spock paused. "The Boqus is standing by its equipment, Captain. All elements of the mechanism are in readiness."

"Position?"

"Still too far away." Not that Kirk had expected any other reply—they would have to draw the dazed jawanda into the trap.

"Captain!" Kirk looked back to Arex. "The creature is turning. It has reversed its direction and is now moving toward us."

"Mr. Sulu, you are aware of the position of the Boquian mechanism?" Kirk inquired hurriedly. The helmsman nodded confirmation. "Change course then, to take us through its center. Continue to slow speed toward warp-factor one."

"Coming about, sir ... slowing."

Long minutes passed, while the jawanda, its thin body still blazing with all the fury of a translucent reactor, expanded on the screen with startling speed. The reason was evident: The *Enterprise* had to change course in a wide curve, while the jawanda had simply folded in on itself, in effect going instantly into reverse.

"It's closing on us, sir," Sulu announced. "Coming on at warp-factor one point ... warp-two." He threw a hasty glance over his right shoulder. "Should I increase our own speed?"

"Steady as she goes, Mr. Sulu," responded Kirk calmly, his eyes never leaving the viewscreen.

A shorter pause, then, "Still gaining rapidly on us, sir."

How beautiful it was, Kirk had to admit to himself.

Rippling, convulsing in smooth arcs of its body, the jawanda enlarged to fill the rear scanners, emitting energy in glowing discharges hundreds of kilometers long. What other inhabitant of the universe, however high, however low, sweated such magnificence?

"Captain," Sulu began worriedly.

"It's all right, Mr. Sulu. Attention to your station." He flicked a look sideways. "Mr. Spock?"

"Another minute yet, Captain."

Kirk considered. The jawanda was almost within contact distance of the ship's warp-drive units. If he accelerated, he chanced discouraging the creature. Or, worse, making it wary. Was it still angry or hungry enough to continue following them, even if he speeded up? Or would it—

"We are within the cage, Captain," Spock announced sharply. "Hivar has activated the mechanism." The first officer watched with interest through the images funneled to him from the Lactrans as Hivar the Toq drew strange sounds and lights from the free-form shape of the Boquian console with smooth movements of many-jointed crystalline limbs.

"Quarry is slowing, sir," reported Sulu. "Showing indications of uncertainty in its pursuit."

"It senses the collapsing gravity wells," Kirk murmured. Was the jawanda capable in its energy-engorged state of breaking clear of the cage?

"Slow to warp-one, Mr. Sulu."

"Reducing speed ... It's beginning to change course, sir."

"Definitely suspicious now," muttered McCoy, staring raptly at the screen. They were about to play out the last act of the drama begun seemingly so long ago, back on the surface of Lactra.

"Full course change," Arex announced, "and it is accelerating."

"Bring us about on a pursuit course, Mr. Sulu ... but slowly. Let's see if it can break free."

The *Enterprise* commenced another wide curve, which would bring it around behind the jawanda again—if Kirk chose to give the order to increase ship velocity, for the energy-eater was now fleeing in the opposite direction.

Kirk knew that if it broke free of the Boquian mechanism they would never be able to approach within capture range again.

"It's slowing, sir," Sulu declared positively. "Slowing . . . It's stopped!"

On the heels of the helmsman's announcement, Spock informed them, "Hivar pronounces itself satisfied as to the mechanism's performance. All six moons have been properly aligned, and the jawanda is trapped by their gravity."

"For how long?" McCoy whispered, gesturing at the screen. "Look."

Twisting and writhing like confetti in a tornado, the jawanda was rushing in tight circles around the inside of its invisible cage. Incredible bursts of pure energy bristled on its surface as it hunted frenetically for a hole in the trap.

Accelerating breathtakingly to warp-three it probed violently at the weakest points of the cage, between the moons. But no matter which way it darted, it could not escape the attraction of at least four of the controlled satellites. The octahedral prison proved secure.

"That's a lot of energy it's throwing off," Kirk noted. "Mr. Sulu, activate our defensive screens." The helmsman touched several switches—not a minute too soon, it turned out, as something powerful shook the bridge. There was a pause and then a second enormous purple bolt of energy crossed the space between ship and jawanda.

"It may not be intelligent," Kirk observed, stilling the slight shaking in his hands, "but it's not blind and helpless, either." He knew the power of the *Enterprise*'s defensive screens, but it was one thing to consider them from the standpoint of abstract statistics and another to do so while looking down the throat of an energy charge as big around as one of the ship's warp-drive units.

As Kirk ordered the cruiser to back off as far as

possible, the madly convulsing jawanda continued to throw harmless if awesome bolts at them.

Spock observed dispassionately, "We already know that the creature is able to transmute great quantities of energy, Captain. It is not surprising that so efficient a converter should be capable of utilizing its ability to discharge excess energy for defensive purposes."

They remained in position while the attacks from the jawanda decreased steadily in intensity.

"Damage report, Lieutenant Uhura?"

"All negative, Captain," she replied. "All decks and stations report no injuries and no damage, although Engineering reports that the first several charges put considerable stress on the defensive screens. Since then, however, they report all attacks shunted aside with ease."

Kirk's attention went once again to the screen. Save for throwing an isolated spark toward the *Enterprise*, the jawanda had apparently given up its assault. Its movements, also, were much subdued. There was no more violent spinning about and contorting. Now it drifted in one place, its black surface rippling slowly like the stomach of an exhausted, overweight man drawing in painful breaths after a long run.

Bright bursts of light continued to show within its great body, but they came in fitful spurts now instead of the regular patterning previously observed.

"We've tired it out, I think," Kirk commented. "Is the Boqus ready to move, Mr. Spock?"

The first officer nodded. "Hivar indicates that the ancient components are performing well. Given a modest amount of power to feed to the control console, it foresees no difficulty in sustaining the cage indefinitely. The Lactrans," he added unnecessarily, "are overjoyed at our success."

"We're not in orbit around Lactra yet," Kirk pointed out. "I'll accept congratulations later. What about the possibility of our prisoner absorbing fresh strength from the radiation we'll encounter once we reenter the denser region of our galaxy?"

"All the energy it could assimilate from passing stars

cannot possibly match the quantity it has already sapped and discharged from the warp-drive engines, Captain," the first officer insisted, after performing several calculations on the ship's computer. "We have already handled its best assault without damage."

"That's all I wanted to know. Mr. Arex?"

"Captain?"

"Plot a course to Lactra, presumably retracing our original tack via Boqu. Mr. Sulu, ahead warp-factor three."

Their acknowledgments sounded simultaneously, and soon the *Enterprise* was again Lactra-bound. Kirk's attention was still focused on their giant captive. He hoped Hivar the Toq was concentrating as intensely on his mechanism. They couldn't dare allow the jawanda even a small chance to escape.

But the octahedral cage formed by the six moons kept the energy-eater locked between them, dragging it smoothly along as they sped back toward the galaxy— although Kirk would have employed a term weaker than "sped," since at warp-three, they seemed to crawl along. But they were restricted to the maximum speed of which the old engines in the moons were capable.

During the following days Kirk had ample time to inspect that remarkable Boquian relic, its peculiar power leads, and the strange broadcast antennas temporarily installed on the epidermis of the *Enterprise*— antennas which somehow carried Hivar's instructions through the shapeless console to the six satellites caging the jawanda.

"Remarkable piece of instrumentation," Spock commented, bending to study the back of the console. It looked no different from the front.

"Prompted by a remarkable need," thought Hivar.

"How was it built?" inquired Kirk, wondering if it would last the duration of the journey back to Lactra.

"I do not know . . . I was able to learn only how to operate it." Hivar's concern mirrored Kirk's own. "The sooner we deposit the creature in orbit around your other guests' home world, the better I will feel, as it will signal the beginning of my return to Boqu."

The intercom buzzed for attention, and Kirk moved to acknowledge the call. "Bulk Transporter Room Three. This is the captain speaking."

"Lieutenant Uhura here, sir." There was an underlying hint of anxiety in that dulcet tone which made Kirk pay closer attention.

"Trouble, Lieutenant?"

"It's not certain, sir. According to Mr. Sulu, the creature is generating an unusual amount of energy. I've confirmed its output with my own instruments."

"You mean it's throwing energy bolts at us again?"

"No, sir." Kirk relaxed considerably, even though they'd already successfully fended off one such attack. "The discharge is in the form of radio waves."

"We already know that the jawanda is capable of producing those, Uhura," Kirk reminded her. "I presume you've detected something out of the ordinary about its present output or you wouldn't have called it to my attention."

"I think so, sir," she said slowly. "The emissions are in short, intense bursts of a type previously unrecorded. I have no idea what significance this holds, if any. But it's such an extreme departure from everything the creature has generated so far that I thought you'd wish to be notified."

"Rightly so, Lieutenant. I've no more idea than you what the meaning of this new activity is." He glanced back toward the attentive Spock.

"Nor have I, Captain," he admitted.

"Keep monitoring the output, Lieutenant," Kirk ordered her, "and begin taping." He flipped off the intercom and looked at the curious Boqus. "You'll have to continue the explanation of the mechanism's history later, Hivar. It's probably nothing, but . . ."

"But what, Captain Kirk?" came the thought, strong and heady.

"It's probably nothing." Kirk decided he was worrying unnecessarily over a harmless new phenomenon, when he had plenty of known dangers to plague himself with. A few moments of study should suffice; then he could dismiss the development from his mind. But those few moments were not to be ignored. Their knowledge of jawandas still bordered on the nonexistent.

On returning to the bridge, Kirk's first instructions were for Uhura to play back some of the noise the jawanda had already produced. As it turned out, recordings weren't required.

"It hasn't let up, sir," the communications officer informed him. "It continues to repeat the same pattern, identically modulated as the initial outburst. Here, I'll put what it's currently broadcasting onto the speakers." Her hands adjusted controls.

An ear-splitting shriek drenched the bridge in bone-grating waves of sound. Kirk's hands went instinctively to his head. That soul-rending howl was piercing his skull over and over. The impression was worse than the actuality, since it was barely a couple of seconds before Uhura could reduce the volume to a bearable level.

"I'm sorry, sir," she apologized contritely. "I thought I'd reduced the level considerably." She eyed an isolated readout angrily. "Here's the trouble—the creature has intensified its output tremendously since I first contacted you." She shook her head in awed amazement. "The amount of energy it's putting out is just incredible, sir."

"I see. Mr. Spock, your opinion?"

Spock concluded his preliminary sensor study of the new emissions and looked up thoughtfully. "Perhaps it is merely another form of energy release, Captain, an instinctive reaction to the unusual situation in which it presently finds itself, akin in spirit if not function to the defensive charges it attacked us with before.

"At first I suspected that the noise might merely be the normal energy discharge of the creature, its intensity the result of all the radiation it had absorbed from the *Enterprise*. Now that I have heard it, I begin to doubt this explanation. My uncertainties are compounded by Lieutenant Uhura's insistence that these discharges are of a type previously not detected." She nodded ready confirmation. "Beyond the normal excretion of surplus energy, I cannot begin to imagine what function these violent pulsations have— Wait ... wait ..."

A clumsy gray shape squeezed out of the turbolift onto the bridge. The young Lactran was already in close communication with Spock.

"The youth is relaying concern from Hivar the Toq," the first officer explained thickly. "The Boqus wishes to hear the sound for itself."

Kirk, picturing the eyeless, earless Boquian scientist, wondered if it "heard" in the same fashion as humans, or if the sound waves were absorbed uniformly across its sensitive crystalline surface. The latter was quite likely. The sound conductivity of crystals was known on Earth as far back as the Dark Ages.

"Pipe the broadcast through to the transporter chamber the Boqus is located in, Lieutenant," Kirk directed Uhura.

Her hands again adjusted controls. "Transporter Room locked into circuit, sir," she replied.

Something about the sound must have been familiar to the Boqus, because Spock's relayed response followed immediately on Uhura's announcement.

"Hivar recognizes the sound, Captain. There are recordings of identical vibrations on Boqu, and although they are extremely ancient Hivar insists the duplication here is unmistakable."

"Duplication of what?"

"A jawanda distress call."

That caused Kirk to pause, all right! There was only one possible corollary, but he asked the question anyway. "Distress call? To—others of its own kind?"

Spock turned to face him, though his gaze remained focused on a point halfway between the command chair and the science station. "Exactly, Captain."

Rapidly Kirk performed some crude calculations in his head, then relaxed slightly. Even if his estimations were a little off, there was still no reason to panic. "We could do without visits from our captive's cousins,

Spock, but, judging from its initial attack, and taking into account that we'll be prepared this time, our screens ought to be able to handle energy charges from a modest swarm of jawandas. Particularly from jawandas who haven't been sucking up energy from our engines. No, I don't see much reason for concern. We're already traveling at warp-three. Even if the calls are picked up, even if a few of the creatures have an intercept angle on us prior to our reentering the galactic field, they'll have only their natural store of energy to draw upon." He started to rise, intending to return to the transporter room to conclude the examination of the Boqus's console.

"Hivar the Toq begs to differ with you, Captain," countered Spock. "Hivar urges that in the event another of the creatures is contacted, we release our captive and accelerate away as rapidly as possible."

A thoroughly stunned Kirk settled slowly back into his chair. "But . . . why? For what reason? My evaluation—"

"The Lactrans are arguing strongly against such a possible course of action," the first officer continued. "Hivar sidesteps. It insists that such an eventuality is unlikely, but that it must be considered."

"I still don't see why." Kirk frowned.

"The Boqus is embarrassed, Captain. It has withheld information, in the manner of the Lactrans, but claims that in this case it was only to"—the first officer strained, trying to translate alien concepts—"spare us needless worry. Hivar now feels that the worry is needful. The Lactrans could not know, but Hivar explains that if the old records are correct, we have captured an immature jawanda."

McCoy spoke for the first time since Kirk and Spock had returned to the bridge. He had remained unusually silent, standing by the engineering station and listening to the strange moans of their captive. But this latest information moved him to comment.

"You mean that monster is a baby?"

"Equivalent terminology has not existed in reference

to jawandas, Doctor, but in the present situation Hivar feels it is appropriate."

"Then how big," McCoy wanted to know—or did he, he wondered—"does an *adult* jawanda grow?"

"No one knows," Spock murmured. There was silence on the bridge.

XI

"Hivar is struggling to recall long-dormant, little-used knowledge, Captain," Spock finally said into the lingering silence. "The estimate of our captive's immaturity is based on such information. The largest jawanda the Boqus were ever forced to drive away was ... a moment ..."

The pause was too much for an impatient McCoy, who soon pressed, "Was what, Spock?"

"Please, Doctor," the first officer cautioned calmly. "I am attempting with Hivar's aid to convert ancient Boquian measurements to Federation equivalents." A longer pause; then he announced firmly, "The largest specimen recorded by the ancients was approximately two hundred ten thousand by fifty-two thousand kilometers. That is only an approximation, remember."

Kirk tried to envision a living creature with a surface area five times that of the Earth and gave up. "That's only the largest the Boqus *know* of. I suppose ..." He hesitated, and the question came out in a whisper. "The possibility exists that there could be larger ones?"

"As a matter of fact," Spock agreed, readily confirming Kirk's worst imaginings, "the planet-bound Boqus theorized from specimens they observed and far-distant radiation they recorded that exceptionally mature jawandas could grow considerably larger."

"How big," the captain queried masochistically, "is 'considerably'?" He was still trying to adjust to the information that the continent-sized energy-eater trailing them was but a midget of its kind.

"Hivar suggests without humor that you use your imagination, Captain. Theoretically, there *is* no upper limit. There are no physiological restraints on a jawanda's growth, and nothing is known of their age. Hivar goes on to say that there is no reason to suppose that, barring a collision with a star, a jawanda could not grow to the size of a sun. Though he reminds us that this is only theory."

"How encouraging," muttered a dazed McCoy.

"Never mind, Spock," declared Kirk suddenly. "I have no desire to tangle with anything even half the size of that old recorded supergiant, whether the Boquian mechanism can shove it around or not. But it will take something that size, which can demonstrate its power, to make us abandon this catch. Because I'm not sure which would be worse—fighting off such an antagonist or starting this hunt all over again, from the beginning." He looked forward.

"Mr. Arex, maintain maximum resolution on all long-range scanners."

"Yes, sir," the navigator replied tersely.

"Lieutenant Uhura, I want you to engage your own long-range detectors and initiate a full-spectrum sweep in the region immediately astern, with regular adjustments to scan every second of sky."

"Monitoring wave sweep, sir," she declared several minutes later.

Kirk's thoughts then turned inward, brooding on ominous possibilities as he studied the viewscreen. Five thousand kilometers of thin organism rippled slowly aft. Listening to the steady, powerful bursts of energy which still sounded over the muted speakers, he considered the history of man's efforts to turn amplified ears to the stars. Little had any of those ancient scientists realized, when they'd fought to make sense of the strange pops and crackles and hums, that among that stellar babble might be the cry of a troubled child.

"It will not be long at our present speed, Captain," announced Spock encouragingly, "before we enter the first fringe star-clusters along our return path into the Milky Way. According to the information imparted by the Boqus, this should be enough to discourage any pursuit."

"How can it be so sure?" wondered McCoy. "The risk of permanent imprisonment, or even death, wouldn't be enough to dissuade a lot of human parents from trying to rescue their offspring."

Spock eyed him reprovingly. "You are anthropomorphizing, Doctor. We cannot ascribe even faintly human or Vulcan motivations to these creatures. They lie outside the boundaries of familiar xenobiology. Besides, it is likely that they reproduce asexually, which renders the parent-child relationship absurd."

McCoy stared at the viewscreen. "I only hope you're right, Spock."

Days passed during which the captured jawanda continued to emit regular cries. It showed no sign of weakening. On the contrary, as they drew near the outer fringe of the galaxy, the outbursts intensified slightly.

Listening closely, Kirk sought to identify something recognizable as a cry for help in those dips and squeaks of electromagnetic radiation. He failed, with a consistency that pleased him. The purely electronic wail enabled him to regard the thing behind the ship as an elemental force of nature instead of a living creature which might possibly possess a glimmer of the thoughts and emotions Spock insisted it did not.

"Captain," Uhura announced slowly, "I think I've got something." Amazing, Kirk mused, how much was contained in that single word, "something."

"It's at the extreme end of my scanners," she went on. "It may be nothing at all, but we're still in intergalactic space, and I thought that——"

"Of course," Kirk cut her off impatiently. "You've isolated it?"

"Yes. It's definitely not a stable intergalactic phenomenon. At first I thought it might be a very small radio nebula—it's definitely generating strong radio pulses. But it wanders about too much. I can't tell yet whether it's moving toward us or not, but . . ." She gazed significantly at Kirk.

"Keep monitoring it, Lieutenant," Kirk instructed her. "Mr. Spock, initiate intensive sensor scan along the coordinates being studied by Lieutenant Uhura. Let me know what you turn up."

"Very good, Captain."

"How much longer before we reach a star with sufficient gravity to hold a jawanda?"

Spock checked library information. "At least another three days at our present speed, Captain, possibly four. Naturally, that time would shrink rapidly at warp-four or warp-five."

Kirk spent a few moments ruminating on their options. "Contact the Boqus, Mr. Spock. Inquire if there's *any* chance, however slight, that the six moons could attain a faster speed."

A short wait, and Spock replied, "Hivar says no, Captain. We might as well abandon the creature now to retain control of the mechanism. The Lactrans are again arguing strenuously. They are willing to jeopardize their lives in order to return the jawanda to Lactra."

"That's noble of them," snorted McCoy, "but what about the rest of us who don't care to stick our necks out so they can add that"—and he gestured toward the screen—"electrified tinfoil to their zoo?"

"Easy, Bones," Kirk advised him, "we're not at that point yet. It may turn out to be just a false alarm."

The alarm was ringing louder the following day. Whatever was generating those powerful pulsations was doing so at a steadily rising rate.

"Estimated distance to the object, Lieutenant Uhura?"

She checked her readouts. "It's still hard to say, sir. The strength of the emissions, and by inference the distance separating us, could vary greatly depending on the size of the creature."

A sinking feeling ran through him. "You're convinced the signals are emanating from another jawanda, then?"

She hesitated. "The differences in the type of pulsations are significant, sir, but the frequencies are identical. Say better than fifty-fifty that it's another."

"An inaccurate observation, Lieutenant," Spock commented mildly. He would never cease to be fascinated by the human tendency to offer approximations in place of absolute figures in matters scientific.

"Let it go now, Jim," urged McCoy. "We'll circle far around and find another specimen for the Lactrans."

"Not yet, Bones. This new arrival—if that's what it turns out to be—may only be curious. Maybe it's not coming in response to the other's cries. We've come too far and worked too hard to give up easily. Remember our obligation to the Lactrans."

"Remember our obligation to the ship."

Kirk threw him a sharp look. "I'm fully aware of that, Bones."

McCoy turned away. "Sorry, Jim . . . Forgot myself for a moment."

"Forget it. We're all operating under stress. The possibility of fighting something that could envelop a few Earths is enough to rattle anyone's thoughts."

What was troubling Kirk was not the chance that another jawanda was the source of the new emissions—that already seemed fairly certain. It was the fact that the mysterious generator was continuing to gain on them—without an intercept angle. It was approaching rapidly from almost dead astern.

That meant that at least some jawandas were capable of moving at speeds above warp-three. Given that, there was no reason to suppose that one of the creatures might not be able to exceed warp-eight—the maximum emergency velocity of the *Enterprise*.

If Spock was right and the jawanda was purely a superefficient energy-converting organism, then it should be as incapable of experiencing the desire for vengeance as it was of feeling parental concern. In that case, it didn't really matter how fast certain jawandas could travel.

On the other hand, if Spock was wrong and the creatures were able to feel higher emotions . . . Kirk refused to consider the possibilities. Long before that he would have to make other decisions.

"It is obvious that we have two choices." Spock pontificated from the science station. "We can retreat at top speed toward the safety of stellar gravity, abandoning our capture in the process, and hope this will be sufficient to discourage any pursuit. Or we can continue as we are and hope that the creature closing on us will become disinterested, give up, or prove unable to hamper our movements."

"Neither of which is an especially appealing alternative," Kirk commented distastefully.

"I concur, Captain. With your permission, therefore, I should like to initiate what is known in human vernacular as a decoy action."

"Decoy?" McCoy echoed. "What are we going to do—have the ship's nonmetallic fabricators make up an artificial jawanda?"

"No, Doctor. I doubt that a visual simulacrum would have any effect. These creatures obviously detect one another by means of their emissions. Sight would be a superfluous sense in the void."

"Go ahead, Mr. Spock," Kirk urged. "Whatever you have in mind can't worsen our situation."

"I hope it can better it, Captain." He faced Communications. "Lieutenant Uhura, have you a precise record of the pattern of the captured jawanda's output?"

"Many, Mr. Spock. Its broadcast has remained consistent, and I've had more than enough time to examine its wave generation in depth."

"How complex is the pattern?" Kirk began to have an inkling of his first officer's plan.

"Not very . . . Oh, I understand. I don't see why our equipment couldn't generate a similar signal, Mr. Spock."

It didn't take long for an emergency engineering and tech crew to ready one of the cruiser's shuttlecraft for a high-speed deep-space run. Lieutenant M'ress supervised the modification of the shuttle's communications equipment, which involved installation of components which would permit the tiny craft to channel far more power than normal into its communications instrumentation.

The hasty alterations completed, the shuttlecraft hangar was cleared and the remotely guided craft launched away at its maximum acceleration. There followed a period of anxious waiting for the shuttle to reach a decent distance from the *Enterprise*. All the while, the source of new radiation drew nearer and nearer.

"Time enough," Spock announced, looking up from his readouts. "Begin broadcasting immediately, Lieutenant Uhura." As she acknowledged, Spock faced the command chair.

"Utilizing the full broadcast power of the *Enterprise*'s communications equipment, Captain, as rebroadcast out into space through the shuttlecraft's modified instruments, we should be able to produce considerably more noise than our captive does. Hopefully, the pursuing jawanda will consider the shuttlccraft's broadcast as the distress call of a second one of its kind. We are hoping that it will opt to aid the louder of the two calls."

Spock's logic, as always, seemed sound. Uhura adjusted her controls, and soon a second jawanda cry for help was filling space, one twice as powerful as the first.

"Captain?"

Kirk looked toward the navigator. "What is it, Mr. Arex?"

"I believe the second creature is changing its course. Indications point to—"

A rhythmic screech drowned him out. Hastily Uhura adjusted her instrumentation once again, and the volume dropped.

"What happened, Lieutenant?"

Uhura studied her gauges and sensor feedbacks. "Apparently our captive has increased the strength of its own radiations, sir. The level is considerably above what we are rebroadcasting through the shuttlecraft."

"Second object shifting direction again, Captain," the soft-spoken Edoan announced. "It is once again following—and it appears to have increased its speed."

Kirk wondered if they could fool their still unknowable pursuer another time, wondered if it felt anger at deception or was simply continuing to follow the strongest signal.

"Increase broadcast power, Lieutenant," Spock directed her.

"I'm sorry, Mr. Spock." Uhura threw him a look of helplessness. "We're broadcasting at maximum strength now. In fact, we can hold this level only another twenty minutes before components begin to melt."

"That won't be necessary, Uhura," Kirk told her. "Maintain power, though. Mr. Sulu, vary the course of the shuttlecraft—random pattern, simulate erratic behavior. Let's see if the second jawanda reacts to that."

"Course still unchanged, sir," Arex reported five minutes later. "Still in pursuit."

Kirk sighed and faced the science station. "It was a good idea, Spock—only it didn't quite work. If we could put more power into our decoy broadcast . . ." He shook his head slowly.

Spock's head tilted at the odd angle Kirk had come to recognize often these past weeks. "Before abandoning the idea, the Lactrans wish to make an attempt of their own." He looked around. "And they want your approval before they do so . . . Doctor."

"Me?" McCoy was taken aback. "Why mine?"

"Because what they wish to try involves a certain amount of discomfort for every member of the crew."

McCoy turned pensive and finally said, " 'Discomfort' is a mild word. Do they think whatever they have in mind could be dangerous?"

A pause while Spock relayed: "They do not think so, Doctor, but admit that they cannot be sure. It is a new thought of theirs, something never before tried, because the opportunity to do so with minds like ours has not previously existed."

Kirk wasn't sure he liked the sound of that. Still, he had to consider the enigmatic threat closing on them every second.

"Bones?"

McCoy looked askance at Kirk. "This is crazy, Jim. How can I estimate the danger when I have no idea what they're going to try?" He turned to Spock again. "You're sure you've got your 'conceptualizations' straight, Spock? They did say 'discomfort' and not 'disablement'?"

"Quite sure, Doctor."

McCoy shrugged. "Then I suppose I can't object."

"All right, Spock," Kirk said warily, "tell them go ahead." He activated the general intercom and explained to the crew as well as he was able what was about to happen. He clicked off finally. "Tell them also that the second we receive any indication that anyone is being seriously affected, they'll have to stop whatever they're doing."

"They understand and agree, Captain," the first officer informed him instantly.

Silence followed. Kirk sat tensely in his chair, waiting for something to happen. When minutes passed and nothing did, an impatient, nervous McCoy asked, "When are they going to begin, Spock? If they don't hurry up . . ."

"They already have, Doctor. They are proceding slowly, so as to be certain they do not hurt anyone— including themselves. Don't you feel it?"

"Feel what, Spock? I don't . . ." Something was whispering inside his head. Irritated, he tried to shake it off, but, like a persistent mosquito, it refused to go away. Instead, it intensified slightly, still irritating but not quite painful. The internal humming became a headache, then a throbbing behind his eyes, relentless and unresolved. He started to speak to Spock, but decided not to when he saw that the first officer was sitting rigidly at attention. The more intensively McCoy tried to analyze the sensation, the more the ache increased.

"Captain," Uhura groaned, holding both hands to her temples, "how much longer does this go on? I can't stand it and monitor the sensors as well."

" 'Discomfort' was the right term, Spock," the captain admitted, wincing. "It's not quite as bad as a migraine—but I hope we're not supposed to endure it too much longer. What are they doing?"

Spock's reply came slowly, since he was speaking under the dual stress of translating and this new mental strain. "They say it will grow no worse. As to the activity itself, the proposal occurred to them when it became clear how limited was the broadcast capability of the *Enterprise*. They are surprised that we did not recognize the presence on board of several hundred additional generators of modulated electrical impulses. The mind of every crew member is such a transmitter.

"It is an ability of all Lactrans to serve as a focusing point for such energies, much as a magnifying lens concentrates sunlight. They are presently utilizing the generative capacity of every mind on board to beam a simulacrum of the jawanda's distress call to the same point in space as the shuttlecraft. The combination of the shuttle's own broadcast and this mental projection may be strong enough to—"

Arex, who alone of the bridge complement seemed relatively unaffected by the Lactrans' activities, made both aliens and science officer into seers: "Captain— our pursuers are changing course once again. They are definitely inclining toward the retreating shuttlecraft, by a significant number of degrees."

Kirk's response struggled through the pounding in his brain. "Lieutenant Uhura, what reaction from our captive?"

"No . . . change, sir," she replied, her expression contorted from the effort of interpreting her readouts. "It's maintaining the same level of broadcast intensity. Maybe it's reached its limits."

"Still continuing on a divergent course, sir," Arex reported. "They are definitely headed away from us now and are beginning to fall behind."

"Thank you, Mr. Arex. Continue close sensor scan

on—" He broke off, rehearing the navigator's recent words. "A moment ago you said 'pursuers,' Lieutenant. There are more than one?"

"It appears likely, Captain. I am tracking three to four sources sufficiently far apart to preclude any other explanation. I thought at first that the one very large creature might be generating signals from various regions of its body, but it seems now that the distance between sources is too great. All, however, are angling toward the shuttlecraft."

Kirk wondered if the relief was visible in his expression. To have one of the monsters closing on them was frightening enough. Three or four ... "Mr. Sulu, how long before we reach the gravity well of a strong sun?"

There was no formal "border" to the home galaxy, cf course. Distances between suns were so unimaginably vast that the term was more suggestive than descriptive. But, compared to the reach of intergalactic space, the gravityless habitat of the jawanda, the region they were about to enter was rich in stars and jawanda-pinioning gravity.

"Twenty-two minutes ship time, Captain," the helmsman finally responded. Kirk's anxiety lightened a little at that encouraging report.

"Keep a close scan on our decoyed pursuit, Mr. Arex. Let me know the instant they show any sign of changing course again. Mr. Spock, can the Lactrans sustain their broadcast for the requisite time remaining?"

"They reply that they will have to, Captain."

Kirk nodded understandingly, his gaze shifting back to the long-range scanner view now on the main screen. It showed only dark, empty space aft of the imprisoned jawanda. For another twenty minutes it had to stay that way.

They crept along at warp-three, Kirk chafing at the restrictions of the Boquian mechanism which forced them to travel at far below normal cruising speed. As the Lactrans had promised, the throbbing grew no worse, but neither did it decrease.

Glancing around the bridge, he saw that Uhura, Sulu, Arex, and even Spock were beginning to show signs of real strain. He heard his own discomfort reflected in the concern in McCoy's voice. The doctor walked over, massaging his temples with slow circular hand motions.

"Jim, even a headache can produce damage if it's allowed to continue untreated. I can't prescribe treatment for something like this."

Kirk checked the official chronometer set in one arm of his chair. "A few minutes more, Bones. We can survive a few minutes more."

Then they would enter the vicinity of NGC 7332. An unremarkable M3 star, hitherto unvisited by anything more complex than a Federation long-range mapping drone. But the cold orange-red giant was a nearing haven for the *Enterprise,* a ten-million-kilometer-wide beacon whose gravity was now akin to the fire with which primitive man had frightened off pursuit by hulking furry carnivore.

He berated himself for falling into the trap McCoy so often entangled himself in, ascribing familiar characteristics to the unfamiliar—in this case the jawanda. That inexplicably efficient inhabitant of deep space was neither furry nor carnivorous.

A shout came from the normally placid navigator's station.

"What is it, Mr. Arex?" he asked quickly. "Have the signal sources changed course again?"

"No, sir." Something in the Edoan's voice sent a tremor along Kirk's nerves. "I have detected a new source of radio emissions. It is larger . . . than all the others combined."

"Bearing?"

"Directly for us, sir . . . warp . . . warp-*seven!*"

"Time to gravitational tangency, Mr. Sulu?"

"Three minutes twenty seconds remaining, Captain," the helmsman shot back.

"The new source is far off, Captain. We should just slip into the safe zone before it reaches us."

"Recalculate for precision," Kirk ordered, thinking in astonishment that that was one phrase he never had expected to direct to his first officer.

"Inconclusive, Captain," Spock replied immediately. "Distance undeterminable at this time."

"Source accelerating!" Arex gasped in disbelief. "Nearing warp-eight!"

"Less than two minutes to go!" shouted Sulu. "Plotting minimum possible orbital radii to maximize gravity effect."

Still nothing on the rear scanners. Where was the apparition? "Emergency magnification on long-range sensors, Mr. Sulu," he directed the helmsman.

Sulu acknowledged, and once more the retreating emptiness jumped perceptibly—to show only a narrower view of nothingness.

"Sixty seconds, Captain."

"Warp-nine, sir," the Edoan said dazedly. "Moving up to warp-ten."

Whatever was after them was now traveling faster than any Federation vessel in existence. It must be converting energy at an incredible rate.

Equally unbelievably, Kirk suddenly felt better than he had in some time. Then he realized that the throbbing in his skull had vanished.

"The Lactrans are aware that their ruse is not discouraging this new, nearer threat, Captain. They see no reason for continuing their broadcast, especially since one of them is verging on unconsciousness and they feel we may soon require our full abilities."

Kirk had time to feel ashamed. While he'd been suffering along with everyone else during the amplified mental broadcast, he'd neglected to consider what toll it might be taking on the amplifiers—the Lactrans themselves.

"Fifteen seconds, sir." Sulu was counting down. "Eleven, ten, nine . . ."

"NGC 7332 in sight on forward scanners, Captain," announced Spock reassuringly. Sulu continued to count off eternities.

"Four, three, two—"

An explosive shriek of outrage and disappointment erupted from every bridge speaker despite Uhura's desperate attempt to reduce it to bearable intensity. Sparks flared from various seals and seams in the communications console, and a small explosion blew out several gauges, the concussion throwing her from her seat. McCoy was at her side in an instant.

"Entering the strong gravitational pull of NGC 7332, Captain," Spock informed him solemnly.

Kirk didn't hear him. He was still seeing something which had appeared for a brief second on the viewscreen, details of its appearance uncertain because the overloaded scanners had automatically blanked themselves out immediately after contacting it.

For an instant something gargantuan had drifted there, filling the screen with discharges of purple and crimson energy whose diameter exceeded that of half a hundred Earths.

Then the scanners came on again and the sun-shape was gone, frustrated, soaring in angry desperation back to the gravitational void of the abyss . . .

"Status, Mr. Spock?" Kirk asked slowly.

"We still retain control of our captive," the science officer assured him. "It seems to have ceased all broadcasting. Undoubtedly it realizes that it has passed the gravitational point of no return."

Kirk swiveled his chair. "Lieutenant?"

Uhura was back on her feet and studying her damaged station with professional concern. "I'm all right, sir. That last outburst—overwhelming." She smiled at McCoy. "Thanks, Doctor." McCoy nodded and moved away, still keeping an inconspicuous eye on her to make sure she was as stable as she claimed to be.

"Hivar the Toq," Spock continued, "states that the mechanism is undamaged and still operating well. We should have no difficulty in retaining control of the captive all the way back to Lactra. The Lactrans are tending to themselves. They are extremely wearied, and the youngster expresses some concern. Both adults are extremely pleased with us. We did not panic, as lower animals would have, and permit the jawanda to escape."

"I'm glad we came up to their expectations," replied Kirk drily. "Continue on course to Lactra at our present speed, Mr. Sulu."

"Aye, sir . . . with pleasure."

"How's your headache, Bones?"

"Completely gone, Jim. No after effects, either." McCoy looked thoughtful. "It occurs to me that the Lactrans' ability to focus the mental output of many minds into various wavelengths could be a powerful weapon."

Kirk agreed. "True, Bones, but I don't think we have to worry about that. Not only aren't the Lactrans a belligerent race, but they'd hardly bother to involve themselves in the petty private squabbles of such primitive creatures as ourselves." He grinned and looked toward the navigator's station.

"Mr. Arex."

"Yes, Captain?"

"Before we entered the gravity well of NGC 7332, I thought we had a momentary view of our pursuer—certainly not extensive enough a glimpse to tell anything. You were monitoring the long-range sensors aft at the time. Did they succeed in recording sufficient information to give us an idea of its size?"

"They did, sir," the Edoan announced slowly. "Quite incredible. It appears that even the Boqus' estimations of the jawanda's upper growth limits were on the conservative side. Were our last pursuer so inclined, and able to withstand the radiation, it could have enveloped Sol."

"No wonder they exist only in intergalactic space," Kirk whispered after a moment's reflection. "They need the room."

McCoy was trying to adjust to the existence of a living organism that size. He could not, naturally. It was beyond the visualizing ability of the human mind. One could write a one and follow it with nine zeros and call it a billion, but the sum could not really be comprehended.

So it was with their final nemesis, an unimaginable colossus turned at the last possible instant by a star trillions of times greater in mass than itself.

From NGC 7332 the journey back to Lactra was mercifully uneventful. Their captive jawanda, now revealed as a true midget of its kind, occasionally testified to its continued health by emitting outbursts of subdued electronic noise.

But it somehow comprehended its position. It made no fresh assaults on the *Enterprise* and did not attempt to flee the gravitational bond of the octahedral cage.

At warp-three the trip back to Lactra took much longer than the journey out, and Kirk and the rest of the crew luxuriated in every minute of it. Eventually, though, the jawanda was installed in polar orbit around that strange world, to circle it forever like some huge foil-shaped moon.

Now fully recovered, the two adult Lactrans and their boisterous offspring were transported back to the surface, though not before confessing that the expedition had enriched their knowledge as well as their zoo.

Thus, free of further obligation to the elephantine superminds, Kirk was able with inexpressible relief to give the order to return at warp-six to Boqu.

Everyone experienced a few moments of apprehension as the *Enterprise* once again left the safety of the galactic arm, apprehension engendered by the fear that a vengeful cluster of mature jawandas might be lingering to ambush them.

But, for all their great size and efficiency at converting energy, the jawandas were the most elemental of organisms, from a mental standpoint. If they possessed minds, these seemed not extensive enough to include memories. The return to Boqu was as peaceful as the race to NGC 7332 had been panicky.

Hivar the Toq and the marvelous Boquian mechanism were returned to the planet's surface, which was still undergoing a burst of activity, thanks to the solution to the pandemic discovered by Dr. McCoy's team.

There was even a remote chance, Hivar assured

Kirk, that Boqu might one day apply for admission as the Federation's farthest-flung member—an eventuality which could be extremely discomforting to such as the Klingons and Romulans.

There was much more to be learned from the sociable Boqus than from the aloof inhabitants of Lactra. In fact, the entire geology section volunteered en masse to remain on Boqu to study the incredible silicon-based ecology. A reluctant Kirk had to deny their applications, for there was no telling when another Federation ship might reach the distant, isolated world.

Leaving the orange-and-mauve storm clouds of Boqu, they returned again to the comforting light of the home galaxy. It was as they were traversing the final stretches of intergalactic void that Spock looked up from his station, wondering aloud.

"One thing continues to prey on my mind, Captain."

"Not fatally, I hope," McCoy quipped.

Spock continued, ignoring the doctor. "We were astonished at the size of the jawanda we captured, only to subsequently discover that it was but an immature specimen of its kind. This was emphasized by the apparent size of its unsuccessful rescuers, who themselves shrank into smallness by comparison with that somewhat larger—"

" 'Somewhat larger,' " McCoy murmured derisively.

"—last pursuer," the first officer concluded, with an admonishing stare at the *Enterprise*'s chief physician. "It continues to occur to me that that final colossus might have its own masters out in the depths of the abyss."

That conception was sufficiently stupefying to silence even McCoy. Together with Kirk, he stared at the view brought close by the ship's after scanners. It was hundreds of thousands of light-years to the nearest pinpoint of light—the outlying stars of Nubecula Major. True, the size of their last pursuer had been unimaginable ... but what was more unimaginable than the vastness of the intergalactic gulf?

"I don't know, Mr. Spock," Kirk mused softly. "Until we encountered the jawandas I'd always been accustomed to thinking of living beings in terms of meters, or, rarely, in thousands of meters. The jawandas have changed that to thousands, maybe hundreds of thousands, maybe even millions of kilometers." He gestured toward the viewscreen. "Perhaps someday we'll encounter creatures out there who'll dwarf the greatest jawanda, and then we'll have to grow used to measuring organisms with light-years instead of metrics."

That was a bit extreme for McCoy. "Now think a minute, Jim, about the impossibility of a living being a light-year in length. Just consider . . . consider . . ." His voice trailed off. "On second thought, I'm not going to consider it right now. One lingering headache in the past couple of months is plenty. I think it's time to consider an extended session in the Rec Room." He left the bridge, the doors of the turbolift closing behind him.

But not before Kirk saw that the doctor's final speculative gaze was focused on the screen and the darkly ominous yet beckoning reaches of the fading intergalactic gulf.